FIRE BOY

J.M. JOSEPH

HODDER CHILDREN'S BOOKS

First published in Great Britain in 2020
by Hodder and Stoughton

1 3 5 7 9 10 8 6 4 2

Text copyright © J. M. Joseph, 2020
Cover and interior illustrations by Samuel Perrett,
© Hachette Children's Group, 2020

A CIP catalogue record for this book is available from the British Library.

ISBN 978 1 44495 468 5

Typeset by Hewer Text UK Ltd, Edinburgh
Printed and bound in Great Britain by Clays Ltd, Elcograf S.p.A.

The paper and board used in this book are made from wood from responsible sources.

Hodder Children's Books
An imprint of
Hachette Children's Group
Part of Hodder and Stoughton
Carmelite House
50 Victoria Embankment
London EC4Y 0DZ

An Hachette UK Company

www.hachette.co.uk
www.hachettechildrens.co.uk

FOR JO PESTEL

a quiz ☑

1. You are handed a box marked **TOP SECRET**. The box is addressed to you. Do you:

A) Rip it open rip it?
Or
B) Wait for your parents to come home before unwrapping it?

If you have answered A, proceed to the next question.
If you have answered B, start again. The correct answer is A.

2. Inside the box you find a jar of sweets and an information booklet. The sweets are labelled **NATURE'S OWN** and smell of peppermint. The information booklet is 48 pages long. Do you:

1

A) Open the jar of sweets?

Or

B) Read page after boring page from the booklet?

If you have answered A, proceed to the final question.

If you have answered B, take a deep breath and read question two again. Then answer A.

3. You discover the sweets unleash a molecular chain reaction. It results in you developing EXTRAORDINARY POWERS. Do you:

A) Run amok, cause havoc at school and join the circus?

Or

B) Master your power, dedicate yourself to a life of public service and become the warrior-hero our world so desperately needs?

If you have answered A, read on.

If you have answered B . . . seriously? B again? It seems you haven't yet twigged how this quiz works. The correct answer is A. NO ONE masters a power from the off. But do not worry, my friend! Help is waiting for you within these very pages. So carry on, and pay close attention.

My name is Aidan Sweeney and I am FIRE BOY.

special delivery

It began with a doorbell.

I was not long in from school. Lemon was curled beside me on the sofa, one white paw tucked under her chin, her tail flung lazily over a cushion. The two of us had the room to ourselves. Mum wouldn't be home for ages and Granny was in her room snoring like a bear.

That was when the doorbell buzzed.

Lemon yawned and rolled over. I sat up.

It buzzed again. This time, a voice from the intercom followed it. 'I have a special delivery for an A. Sweeney.'

A. Sweeney?

A special delivery FOR ME?

The voice spoke again. 'I need you to sign for it.'

I bolted off the sofa, hurdled a stool and skidded to a halt at the doorway. 'I'll be right down!' I yelled into the speaker.

4

Fizzing with excitement, I ran into the hall and pressed the button for the lift.

And yet . . . it was hard not to be suspicious. Who could have sent me a parcel? No one had mentioned a present to me and my birthday wasn't until May. As I rode down to the ground floor, I mulled over the possibilities and weighed their odds.

Mum

Unlikely. Mum believed in rewards, not surprises. None of my most recent accomplishments – coming third in a Longest Spit contest or beating Hussein not once, but twice at *FIFA* on his own Xbox, fell into her 'Achievement' category.

Granny

Hardly. Granny didn't do presents. Granny gave orders. She issued threats and restricted privileges. She handed out punishments like they were fairy cakes at a party. Granny buy *me* a present? Not a chance.

Mitchell Mulch

The favourite. This fell into the 'It's a trick' category. Could Mitchell Mulch be hiding in the bushes with a Super Soaker Double-Pump AK-47 Attack Gun? Very possibly. This 'delivery person' and the surrounding area must be approached with great caution.

It was my lucky day.
The longshot. Fingers crossed.

I burst into the lobby and spotted a thin man in cycling shorts outside the glass partition. He had a Deliver-O box strapped to his back and smallish parcel in one hand. A bicycle leaned against the wall behind him.

My heart went pitter-patter, pitter-patter. This was no trick. This was real.

I rushed to the door and opened it.

'I'm Aidan Sweeney! We just spoke on the intercom.'

The delivery man frowned. Instead of handing me the parcel, he pulled it away. 'I was expecting someone older.'

I made myself as tall as I could – which, in fairness, wasn't that tall. 'I happen to be much older than I look, my good man,' I said in a deep voice. 'If you check the box, you will discover that is my name on the label.'

'I don't know,' he said, scratching his chin uncertainly. 'Do you have any ID?'

'Just this,' I said. Removing one of my trainers, I showed him its heel, where the name *A. Sweeney* was written in a black marker. He held the trainer gingerly, his nose wrinkling.

'Guess that'll do.' He shrugged. 'Here.'

I scratched my name across his electronic pad and he handed me the package.

It was an odd-shaped lump wrapped in brown paper. Postmarks blotted one corner and rows of blue airmail stickers crowded another. One stamp showed a llama in profile. The second, two ponies on a grassy mountain top. The handwriting I didn't recognise – a scrawl of loops in purple biro – but the address was mine: Alexandria Apartments, London, N1.

'Do you know who sent this?' I asked the Deliver-O man, but when I looked up, he had already cycled away. In his place was a girl in a maroon blazer and straw boater.

Sadie was home.

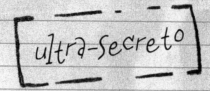

ultra-secret

'You never told me you had family in South America, Aidan.'

'I don't.'

'Then who sent you this?'

Sadie and I were sitting on the sofa back in my flat. Lemon, the traitor, was stretched across Sadie's lap, one eye on the parcel wedged between us.

Four phrases (in no particular order) that best describe Sadie Laurel-Hewitt, aged twelve:

– Tall, long-haired, quick to smile, skilled at football, piano, dance and kick-boxing

– Youngest daughter of the film and television actor, Alice Laurel

– Speaks four languages, unrivalled in board games involving planning, word skills or precision

– Day student at Lady Pandora's School for Girls
and fellow resident of Alexandria Apartments

Sadie pointed to the llama stamp. 'This was posted in Peru. How curious. Are you going to open it or wait until your mum comes home?'

Waiting had never crossed my mind. My only worry was Granny. At any minute, the She-Bear might stumble out of her bed-cave. If she did, I could kiss this parcel goodbye. Granny would snatch it away and what would I be left with? A stiff wallop over the head for daring to answer the door.

I picked up the parcel. 'Trust me. Mum would want me to open it.' Carefully, I tore around the stamps and postmarks – those I wanted to keep. The rest I ripped apart.

Underneath the brown paper was a cocoon of tape. There was no way I could unravel that.

'Do you have any scissors?'

'No,' Sadie said. 'Though this might be useful.' She undid her satchel and pulled out a small bundle of cloth, unknotting it to reveal an arrowhead with a tip as sharp as an eagle's talon. 'Mummy got it for

9

me in America. What do you think?'

'Think?' I stared into her satchel. 'I think you Lady Pandora's girls know how to pack a school bag. What else do you keep in there? Pistols? Grenades?'

'I meant, is it too sharp? I don't want to damage what's inside.'

'It's perfect,' I said, handing her the package. 'You do it.' There was only one person in the room who could be trusted with an object that sharp and it wasn't me. 'I like my fingers as they are – attached to my palms.'

Sadie shifted over. Nudged awake, Lemon took one look at the arrowhead poised over her head and sprang off the sofa, retreating to the armchair where she could watch us in safety.

Gripping the parcel tight, Sadie cut through the tape in one go. She peeled the clumps away. Underneath was a layer of bubble wrap, which she tore off, leaving a small square box with two words stamped in scarlet letters across its top: *ultra-secreto*.

Sadie gasped.

'*Ultra-secreto* means "top-secret"!' Sadie turned to me, her brown eyes burning with curiosity.

'Aidan, who sent you this?'

That was a very good question. I didn't know anyone who lived in South America. I turned the box over. On its back was another stamp: *Propiedad del Laboratorio Cambio*.

My heart sank. 'This must be a mistake. No one would ever send me anything important.' Groaning, I threw myself face-first on to the sofa and began to sob.

By my standards, I was masking my disappointment well.

'Who says it's not for you?' Sadie asked.

I removed my face from the sofa cushion and rolled over. 'What do you mean?'

She shot me a smile and arched her eyebrow. 'It has your name on it, doesn't it? So it's for you. Why worry over who sent it? Let's see what's inside.'

Tips on how to get along with others #1:
It is often helpful to tell your friends exactly what they want to hear.

Who was I to argue? Sitting up, I gripped the box by its lid. 'Ready?' I asked.

'Ready.' Sadie snapped her fingers flamenco-style and clicked her heels. '*¡Abre la caja!*' she cried.

'Tacos! Nachos! Tapas!' I replied in my best Spanish.

And then the doorbell rang. Again.

The Death Star

It was Hussein.

'I want a rematch,' he said, flashing his *FIFA Gold Edition* disc. 'You got lucky. It won't happen again.'

'Twice. I got lucky twice,' I said, following him into the sitting room.

Four phrases (in no particular order) that best describe Hussein Aziz, aged twelve:

– Fan of the films, comics, action masks, collectible toys and other paraphernalia associated with the *Star Wars* series
– Long-limbed, dark-eyed gaming enthusiast and electric guitarist (novice grade)
– Fellow classmate at Caversham School, 2nd Form, and resident of Alexandria Apartments, 4th floor
– Poor loser on *FIFA Gold Edition* for Xbox

Sadie waved him forward. 'Hussein! Come in! You're just in time for the unveiling.' She told him about the parcel as I, its proud owner, stood by smugly.

Hussein did not share our enthusiasm.

'You can't open that,' he said. 'It's against the law to open someone else's post.'

'It's addressed to me, Hussein.'

'That's clearly a mistake. Why would anyone send you top-secret information? You don't know anyone in South America, do you?'

'So?' -

Hussein dabbed his brow. 'You can't take a chance, Aidan. Lives are at stake.'

'Lives?' Sadie rattled the box at him and laughed. 'How? Is there a nest of vipers in here?'

'No,' Hussein said. 'Vipers would never survive the packaging. They'd suffocate.'

'Good,' I said. 'I never liked snakes. Let's open it.'

'But it might contain a deadly virus so contagious it wipes out life as we know it!'

I was beginning to regret opening the door for him.

Sadie stared at him. 'A virus that ends life as we

know it? Inside the box I'm holding? Are you serious?'

'If it gets me out of my maths exam next Tuesday,' I shrugged, 'I'm all for it.'

'This is no joke,' Hussein warned. 'You have no idea what type of top-secret weapon there might be in here. It could be a weapon of mass destruction.' Brow dark with gloom, he scowled. 'Or worse.'

'Worse?'

'You heard me.'

'What's worse than mass destruction?'

Hussein shook his head grimly. 'You don't want to know.'

'Hussein, this isn't the *Return of the Jedi*,' Sadie sighed. 'We're not going to find the plans to the Death Star inside Aidan's box.'

'As a matter of fact,' Hussein crowed, 'the plans to the Death Star *could* be in this box. They were lost and stolen many times, often turning up in the most remote planets in distant galaxies. But would our technology be able to decipher them – that's the question! Do you remember when—'

Sadie stood. 'Aidan, open it now or I'm leaving.'

I hopped over the sofa, landing on the cushion

15

with a thump. I placed the box on my lap and tapped the seat beside me.

Sadie sat down.

'My name is on the package, Hussein. If you or Princess Leia have a problem with that, I'm sorry. But I am opening it anyway.'

Hussein tapped his *FIFA Gold Edition* case nervously against his leg.

'Come on,' Sadie said. 'You don't fool me, Hussein. You want to see what's in here as much as we do.'

This time, Hussein didn't argue. I shifted over and he plopped down next to me.

I opened the box.

A round glass jar and a small green booklet were inside.

I removed the jar.

Through the glass I could see ten jellied sweets dusted with frosting. Each sweet was as plump as a strawberry and had liquorice laces looped around its sides. A white label with green lettering in Spanish and English was stuck to the jar. The half in English said:

NATURE'S OWN

HAND-MADE SWEETS FROM
THE CLOUD FORESTS OF PERU

I turned the jar round.

On the back there was a drawing of a

17

bare-chested warrior in a tall, feathery cap. Underneath him was more writing.

'Nature's Own is a non-profit organisation,' I read aloud. 'Located on the grounds of Cambio Laboratories, Nature's Own chooses only the very best ingredients from its world-famous gardens and greenhouse for our products. Earnings are then channelled into environmental research on behalf of our planet, which is why we say: SAVE THE WORLD – BUY A SWEET!'

'I like the sound of that,' Sadie said.

'Me too.'

Hussein shifted uneasily in his seat. 'Is there a card inside the box telling you who sent it?' he asked.

'No, just this.' I picked up the green booklet and read the first page from *Cambio Laboratories: A Handbook*.

Cambio Laboratories

Our world needs to change. Environmental neglect, a lack of sustainability and the rapid depletion of natural resources are threatening our existence.

At Cambio Laboratories, we are working to reverse this trend. Our labs are based within the cloud forests of Peru, a unique ecosystem which provides researchers with havens of rare trees and plants to study. Here, in the shadows of the Ancient Inca temples at Machu Picchu, scientists combine 21st century technology with the long-lost folklore of our ancestors. For humanity to move forward, we must reconnect with the ways of our distant past.

I flicked through the rest of it. There were another forty-eight pages of this stuff. Chapter after chapter on Peruvian vegetation and the future of botany, all of it in small print. It could take me days – weeks – to get to the end of this.

I tossed the booklet on to the sofa.

'Well?' Hussein asked. 'What does it say?'

I held the jar and shook it. 'These sweets come from cloud forests in Peru. I guess that's what makes them special.'

Hussein wasn't convinced.

'There's nothing "top-secret" about that.' He picked up the box and turned it over suspiciously. 'Why would anyone need to sign for a jar of sweets?'

'Maybe it's a publicity stunt, a way to get people talking about a new line of sweeties and lucky me just happened to get one. So,' I said, pausing to unscrew the lid, 'who wants one?'

'I do,' Sadie said, holding out her hand.

'Are you sure they're safe to eat?' Hussein asked.

I turned the jar over and showed him the sticker on its bottom. It said:

THESE SWEETS ARE SAFE TO EAT.

That stopped his grumbling. 'Okay,' Hussein nodded. 'Give me one.'

When I lifted the lid off the jar, the three of us got a whiff of a cool green forest. Lemon reappeared, sliding along the edge of the sofa, her whiskers twitching. She rubbed against my leg, keen on getting her nose inside the jar.

I fished out three sweets and shared them round. Lemon watched.

'You first, Aidan,' Sadie said. 'They are yours, after all.'

'If you insist.' I held a jellied mint high over my mouth and then let it drop in, catching the sugary-sweet frosted icing on my tongue. I chewed. It tasted of liquorice and peppermint pine, like a sliver of icy mint sliding deliciously down my throat. Seeing me smile, Sadie and Hussein popped their sweets into their mouths.

Cheek bulging, Sadie lisped, 'Thith ith thuper.'

But there was a surprise waiting for us. A hard, round nut was hidden inside the mint. When I bit into it, a fruity juice squirted out, bitter and sweet.

Hussein, who was chomping away for all he was worth, was the next to reach it. 'Oh,' he said.

Sadie wasn't long behind him. Puckering her lips, she said, 'I wasn't expecting that.'

None of us were.

Or what happened next.

where there's smoke...

I got the hiccups.

Yes, that's right. Hiccups.

I know what you're thinking. *Hiccups? What's strange about that? Everybody gets the hiccups.*

True. But they don't often breathe out smoke when they hiccup, do they? Because that's what I did.

The first hiccup was tiny. As I opened my mouth, a small ribbon of smoke spewed from my nose.

'Hic,' I chirped again. This time two thin clouds of smoke streamed out of my ears, hovering over the sofa.

'Hic!' Now three puffs appeared from my mouth one after another, like balls of smoke shot out of a cannon. For the second time that afternoon, Lemon leapt off the sofa and headed for the door.

Hussein buried his head in his hands. 'I knew it,'

he whimpered. 'I knew it. I knew something like this would happen.'

Smoke continued to chimney out of my ears and mouth. 'I think it's that tikka masala I had for lunch,' I said.

Sadie waved the clouds away with both hands. 'Drink some water, Aidan. It might stop the smoke and the hiccups.'

'Good idea!' I cried, bolting towards the kitchen.

'And be quick about it!' Hussein said. 'Before you set off every smoke alarm in the building!'

Sticking my head under the tap, I slurped away for all I was worth. Eventually, the hiccupping stopped. But I had only managed to divert the smoke. Instead of coming out of my nose and ears, now the smoke was billowing out of my bottom and widening into rings that hung over the kitchen table like doughnut-shaped rain clouds. This I found greatly entertaining, especially when my aim improved and I discovered that I could, with a little effort, direct these smoke rings at targets. Clearly, this was a trick in need of an audience, so I rushed out to show Sadie and Hussein.

A proper shock was waiting for me.

Sadie was sitting legs crossed guru-style on our sofa, palms up, eyes closed. Her long hair rippled backwards like it was being blown by a gentle breeze and it sounded like she was chanting. A crown of light surrounded her head like a halo.

'Sadie?' I tapped her knee. 'Sadie? Are you all right?'

Before she could answer, a bang sounded behind me.

It was Hussein.

Gripping the arms of his chair, he sat bolt upright, eyelids fluttering, teeth chattering, feet drumming the floorboards. His straight black hair stood on end, while blue sparks shot off the tips of his fingers as if a thousand megavolts were shooting through him.

Seeing my best friends like this – one shining like an angel in a spotlight and the other shaking like he'd got his toe stuck in a socket – a flood of emotions overwhelmed me.

A brief analysis of the emotional turmoil I was experiencing at this difficult time:

— *Sharp pangs of GUILT.* Because of me, my friends were in danger

— *A worrying CONCERN for my own safety.* Hussein I could handle, but if I upset Sadie, I could be in for a hiding

— *Severe DISAPPOINTMENT.* Neither of them could see my lovely smoke rings and my bottom was running out of puff

— *And, most of all, the crippling ache of REGRET.* Where was my phone when I needed it? I should be videoing this!

By the time I found my mobile wedged under the chair cushion, the light surrounding Sadie had faded. Her long hair fell back into place and her legs dropped to the floor. Her eyelids flickered open.

Hussein returned to near-normal too. Legs slack, his glasses clinging to his nose and his arms still shaking, he slumped backwards in a daze.

'Sadie!' I cried. 'You will not believe what happened!'

Sadie blinked. 'Aidan . . . is that you?'

'Of course, it's me! Are you all right?'

Sadie took a deep breath and exhaled. 'I feel . . . at peace. Like a great wave swept me away and left me at one with the sea and the sky.'

'I can top that,' I beamed. 'A minute ago, I was blowing smoke rings out of my bum. Sorry you missed that, aren't you?'

'Devastated.' Smoothing out the wrinkles in her maroon skirt, Sadie glanced over my shoulder at Hussein. He sat slouched in the armchair, his eyes spinning and his mouth open. His hair was a tangle of clumps and tufts, like he'd been hit by a few bolts of lightning and then walloped over the head with a hammer.

'Oh. My. God,' Sadie said. 'What happened to him?'

I explained what I'd seen in great detail, exaggerating here and there for effect. Sadie gaped at Hussein with alarm. 'Has he said anything yet?' Sadie asked.

'No.'

'Do you think he's all right?'

'Hussein? He's fine. I think he just wants a minute to himself,' I said, lowering my voice. 'You know, a little time to collect his thoughts.'

'Aidan, his tongue is blue and there's dribble coming out of his mouth. He does *not* want a moment alone.' Sadie bit her lip. Her brow puckered. 'We should call a doctor.'

'A doctor? Don't be ridiculous!' I said, opening the jar of Nature's Own. 'Come on. I want to try another.'

That roused Hussein from his stupor. Leaping out of the chair, he threw himself at me hollering, 'ARE YOU CRAZY? Put those away!'

Hussein laying his hands on my neck didn't bother me. We wrestled all the time.

There was no need to shout though.

'AIDAN!' came the roar from the back bedroom.

Granny had woken.

the She-Bear

Hussein let go of my shirt. 'Sorry, Aidan,' he said.

'It's not your fault,' I sighed. 'She had to wake sooner or later.'

'I KNOW YOU'RE OUT THERE!'

From the back bedroom came the snap, crackle and pop of old bones stirring.

'You had better go.'

'Good idea,' Hussein said. Picking up his *FIFA Gold Edition* case, he straightened his glasses and, as best he could, his hair. 'See you tomorrow.'

'See you,' I said as he scooted out the door.

Sadie stood too. She picked up her satchel. 'Aidan?'

'Yes?'

'Promise me you won't eat another one of those sweets.'

'Why?'

'Just don't, not until we're sure they're safe.'

Sadie slung her school bag over her shoulder. 'Something's not right about them.'

'If you say so.' I knew better than to argue with Sadie. If she said trouble was coming, look out. That girl could smell *Danger* before it snuck up and bit you on the backside. I've lost count of the times she's stopped me from being flattened by a bus, falling down an elevator shaft or stampeded by an angry donkey on a trip to the City Farm. When she has a hunch, I listen.

'BOY! WHO'S OUT THERE?'

Sadie picked up her straw boater. 'Aidan, do you feel . . . different?'

'How do you mean?'

'Tingly. Like you've had a good scrub, but on the inside.'

I nodded. I *did* feel different, though it was no gentle tingle. It was more like a volcano had erupted in my stomach, spilling lava left and right. The strange thing was, instead of it making me want to sling ice down my gullet, this fire felt *good*.

From the back bedroom, there came the heave and sigh of a mattress. Bed-boards groaned. Granny was rising.

'BRACE YOURSELF! I'M COMING!'

'Good luck,' Sadie whispered. She walked briskly to the front door and slipped out with a quick wave, easing it shut behind her.

Thump, creak. Thump, creak. Thump, creak, the floorboards warned.

Granny was close.

I slid the delivery box under the table and covered the jar of Nature's Own with its wrapping. I sat back on the sofa and mentally prepared myself for the challenges ahead.

First her walking stick appeared, followed by a brawny fist and then her monstrous head.

'YOU!' she roared when she spotted me.

'Granny!' I said cheerfully. 'This is a surprise.'

'Oh, ho! A surprise, is it?' she said, slamming her walking stick down. 'Well, we will see about that.'

Four phrases (in no particular order) that best describe Granny, aka Hilda Sweeney, aged sixty-four:

- Wide-necked, broad-backed, large-armed, thick-thighed
- Irritable, prone to fits and rages, hoarder of phones, books, games and comics

- Former women's prison officer, avid supporter of rules and discipline, and keen administer of punishment in all its forms
- Resident of Alexandria Apartments, 3rd floor, and current occupier of my former bedroom

Leaning against the armchair, Granny twirled her walking stick with menace.

I backed away. Yes, she was old, but there was more hard muscle on her than Hercules in his prime. In her hands, that cane was like Thor's hammer, a lethal weapon she used to prod, poke, trip and bash. As for the bad knee Granny claimed to suffer from, only a fool would believe that; that stick was a ruse, her way of arming herself for battle. Put Granny in a wrestling ring with a grizzly bear and I know who I would bet on.

'I heard voices,' she snarled. 'Who was it?'

'No one, Granny. Just friends.'

'Friends?' Granny sneered. 'It was those two toe-rags, the girl with the hair and the small boy in glasses, wasn't it?'

I bristled. I wasn't sure what a toe-rag was, but it didn't sound pleasant and, as soon as she put that stick down, I was determined to defend my friends' honour. For now though, I brooded in silence.

'You know the rules: no one is allowed in this flat without asking . . .' Granny stopped. Her nostrils flared and one eye began to twitch. She slammed her walking stick down on the ground and shook her meaty fist. 'I smell smoke! What have you been doing?'

'Me? Nothing!'

'Don't lie to me.' Granny hobbled closer, sniffing me like a crazed bloodhound. 'There's a stink of smoke coming off you.'

'That must be Lemon you're smelling,' I said, scrambling away from her.

'It's not the cat, stupid boy! It's you!' Narrowing her eyes, Granny glared at me. 'You and your friends were smoking my cigars, weren't you?'

'No, Granny. Never!'

'You better not have,' Granny said, poking my chest with the end of her stick and sneering. 'Because if I find one of my cigars missing, it's lockdown. You'll be an old man before you're allowed to leave this flat.' She scowled at me once more and stomped off to the kitchen.

Relieved to see the back of her, I closed my eyes, grateful for a few moments' peace.

It didn't last.

Hearing a strange hissing sound, I opened my eyes. Steam, I discovered, was trickling out of my hands.

My palms glowed red. Cracks of light emerged from my fingertips.

A fierce burst of heat came next, almost knocking me off my feet.

I trembled, unable to believe my eyes.

My hands were on fire.

hands of fire

No science class, no television documentary, no comic book could have prepared me for this.

Each of my hands, from my wrist to my fingers, glowed ember-red. Yellow and orange flames ripped out through my skin, licking the edges of my palms. When I made a fist, my hands became pure balls of fire, one blazing at the end of each arm.

And it didn't hurt!

But how?

The flames were real. I was certain of that. The heat coming off my hands was intense. Already the cuffs of my sleeves were black and fraying. I tried putting out the fire by rubbing my palms together, but that only made the flames flare higher.

What was I to do?

Questions stormed around my head, loud and urgent, demanding answers and receiving no reply, the most important of which was: what was Granny going to say when she saw me like this?

The She-Bear once grounded me for leaving a dirty sock on the sitting-room floor. That meant no TV for two weeks, early bed, and drills at dawn – me struggling to do a single push-up while Granny barked for a hundred more. I was in no hurry to find out what hands of fire might get me. I needed to put those flames out *now*.

The kitchen door burst open. 'BOY!' Granny bellowed.

I raced down the hallway away from her with my flaming hands out in front of me – not the easiest way to run, I'll have you know – so she couldn't see them.

'Oh, ho! Want to play, do you?' Granny called to me. 'There's nothing I like more than a game of "Hunt the Runaway".'

The door to the bathroom was closed, which left me stumped. How do you open a door with flaming hands and NOT set fire to it?

'Hide, boy. Hide yourself well,' the She-Bear cackled from the sitting room. 'Make me work. There's nothing like a little exercise to stir the blood.'

I poked at the handle with my elbows, but couldn't lever the door open.

Granny thumped her walking stick down. 'One!' she bellowed.

The more desperate I became, the fiercer my hands burned.

'Two!'

Somehow, I had to force that door open before . . .

'Three! Here I come!'

An Immoveable Object (the door to the bathroom) barred my way ahead while an Unstoppable Force (Granny and her walking stick) blocked me from behind. It was at this moment of crisis that *Wrestling World* came to my rescue. Only two days ago I had watched Hector 'the Assassin' Morales dispatch Davy 'the Body' Franklin – and the referee to boot – with his trademark move, the 'Scorpion', a flying headbutt swiftly followed by a karate kick to the groin.

If that couldn't open the bathroom door, nothing would.

I took a running start and launched myself into the air Hector Morales-style: arms wide, head back like an angry stag with a point to prove, one leg high and poised to strike.

WHAM!

The door opened, though not as I intended.

My karate chop was lethal, but off-target; I hit the door-frame rather than the door, painfully stubbing my toe. That threw me off-balance, which turned my mighty headbutt into a quite painful face-splat. As I slid down the door, semi-conscious and seeing stars, my shoulder somehow undid the door handle. The weight of my body pushed the door open.

Job done.

Except in all the confusion, I'd forgotten my hands held two small bonfires. Reaching out to stop myself from falling, I knocked over the houseplant Mum kept in the bathroom. That plant, a fern with leaves that hung over its vase in leafy spirals, caught fire, along with a Scooby Doo towel, a bath-mat and Mum's shower cap.

From the hallway came another thump of a walking stick. 'There's no escape, runaway!' Granny shouted. 'I've got you cornered!'

Oh boy.

I wandered lonely as a houseplant

The bathroom door burst open. Granny stomped in and glared at me.

'Boy, what are you doing?'

The air was thick with steam. Sprays of water drummed off my head and back from the overhead nozzle. 'I'm taking a shower,' I snorted. 'What does it look like I'm doing?'

Granny's mouth opened and shut. Her hairy eyebrow, a line that stretched from ear to ear, teetered and fell.

'Is something wrong?' I asked innocently.

Granny scratched her whiskers. Her black eyes narrowed. An emotion I did not usually associate with Granny – concern – crossed her craggy features.

'Have you had a knock to the head, boy? Fallen down some stairs?'

'No, Granny,' I said.

'Had a fever recently? A fit?'

'No.'

'Heard voices talking to you in the night?'

'No.'

Granny gripped her walking stick with both paws and leaned forward. 'Good. Then perhaps you can explain to me why you're showering with your clothes on?'

'Clever, isn't it?' I said, soaping the leg of my trousers. 'I'm doing the laundry *and* scrubbing myself at the same time.'

Granny shuffled forward, inspecting the floor of the tub. 'Why is your mother's houseplant in the shower?

At my feet, the sodden fern dripped and sagged. 'It looked lonely.'

'Lonely?'

'It seemed sad sitting by itself on the shelf.'

Granny tapped the rim of the tub with her walking stick. 'What about the towel and mat? Were they lonely too?'

'Don't be silly, Granny. Towels don't get lonely.'

Granny scowled. 'You are a strange and foolish boy, Aidan. I will have strong words with your mother when she comes home tonight.'

'Yes, Granny.'

'Turn that water off and remove your mother's shower cap. You look ridiculous.'

'Yes, Granny.'

'You are a disappointment to me, boy,' Granny snapped. 'Before your mother comes home, I want this bathroom tidied – it should be spotless, do you understand?'

'Yes, Granny.'

Granny hobbled closer to the tub. 'And don't think I've forgotten our game,' she sneered, jabbing me with her walking stick. 'You've been found, prisoner. You owe me hard labour.'

'Yes, Granny.'

Head bowed, I waited until the door shut before I looked up.

That was close!

Once Granny was gone, I plucked up the courage to examine my fingers.

Would you believe it? There wasn't a single mark – no burns, no scars, nothing!

It was a miracle!

I turned my hands over and counted each finger.

They were all there! It was AMAZING! Relieved, I sprawled out of the shower and collapsed on to the floor. Lemon padded in and meowed, rubbing her head against my knee. Cradling her in my lap, I stroked the soft fur under her ears and, for a short time, tried to forget about hands of fire, top-secret sweets and mad grannies.

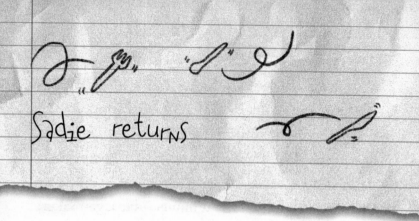

Sadie returns

I closed my school notebook and checked the clock.

Again.

Another hour until Mum was home.

I cleared away my plate and knife and scrubbed the last of the baked-bean sauce out of the pot. Watching me from the counter-top, Lemon stopped flicking her tail. Her ears perked up.

Chook-chook. Chook-chook.

I knew that call.

Chook-chook. Chook-chook.

I raced to the back window and threw it open. There, crouched on the steps of the fire escape, was Sadie.

'Aidan! We must talk. Is it safe?'

'Come in,' I said, helping her inside. 'Granny won't be back until late.'

Tuesday was Darts Night and – HURRAH! – that meant Granny was out for the evening. Her team, the Battle-Axes – Jane Barrow, care nurse at Sleepy Hollow's Home for the Elderly; Mrs Thornhill, headteacher at Our Lady of Sorrows Primary School; Frau Wimmer, sausage-maker; and Mo Muckle, owner of Granny's local, The Anchor – were two-times champions of the Kentish Town Darts League and determined to lay waste to their competitors for a third year running.

'Is your mum home?' Sadie asked.

'Not yet. Why?'

Sadie grabbed me by the arm and pulled me into the kitchen. 'Aidan. Something strange is happening to me.'

'You too?'

'Watch.' Sadie held her hand out over the counter-top. As she did, the dishes drying in their rack began to rattle. Forks shook, spoons wobbled. Knives juddered in their place. The dish towel I'd tossed over the tap wrinkled and flapped. Lemon, who was watching from her perch on the counter, stood and blinked, her back arched.

'How are you doing that?'

Jamming her hands into the pockets of her hoodie, Sadie flopped into a chair and sighed. 'I don't know. That's the problem. As soon as I stare at an object, it moves!'

'It could be worse,' I said.

'How?'

I held my hand out, palm up. It glowed red, then burst into flames.

Sadie jumped back. 'Aidan! Quick! Stick your hand under the tap!'

'I don't need to,' I said, as flames rippled across my fingers. 'It doesn't hurt.'

Her mouth fell open. 'But how?' She warmed her hands over my burning fingers. 'That's a proper fire!'

'I know. I nearly burnt the kitchen down making myself tea. But at least I figured out how to turn it off.' I squeezed my palms together and the flames faded until they disappeared.

'It's those sweets,' Sadie said. 'It has to be.'

She was right. Strange things began happening to us the minute we popped them into our mouths. 'Now we know why that box came with a "top-secret" stamp.'

'True. But who sent it?'

Sadie looked thoughtful. 'Maybe we should have another look at that information book. There might be a clue in there.'

We went into the other room and pulled the box out from under the sofa. The booklet was still there, hidden along with the jar beneath the clumps of Sellotape. When I pulled it out, it seemed as if the Inca warrior on its cover was smirking at us.

We flicked through the booklet, stopping at a page with *Cambio Laboratories: A New Generation of Explorers* written across the top. Underneath the heading, there was a photograph of a group of men and women at the edge of a forest. A smiling, grey-haired man in a red shirt stood in front. Beneath the photo, it said: *Ricardo Sanchez and the research team at Cambio Laboratories.*

Twenty-five per cent of the world's medicines are derived from plants found in rainforests and surrounding areas. Despite this enormous contribution to the health of the human race, little is still known about the fauna that inhabit this habitat. Estimates suggest that fewer than ten per cent of these plants have been tested to determine their possible benefits to our health and welfare.

Cambio Laboratories is committed to addressing this imbalance. Led by the world-renowned botanist, Ricardo Sanchez, our scientists are committed to discovering the healing, nutritional and life-changing properties of the herbs, plants and trees that grow within the cloud forests of Peru.

Sadie frowned. 'A "world-renowned botanist" does not spend his days making jellied mints.'

I leaned closer to look at the photo. As I bent over the booklet, tiny flames sprouted from each of my fingertips.

'Careful!' Sadie cried, flinging the book off her lap before it caught fire. Instead of falling to the floor, it flapped its covers and rose into the air. We watched it glide around the room, its pages fluttering.

'How are you doing that?' I asked.

'I wish I knew,' Sadie said.

The booklet swooped low, forcing us to duck. It missed the top of my head, but nicked the back of the chair. Clattering to the floor, it fell open on a page titled *The Mystical Trees of South America*.

And that's how Sadie and I discovered the hidden message.

El Árbol de los Dioses

There were three mystical trees of South America described on the page.

First was *La Chakana* or 'World Tree' which had roots in the underworld, a trunk which encompassed the earth and branches that supported the heavens. Underneath a drawing of *La Chakana*, there was a long paragraph explaining the origins of the legend and its significance.

La Lupuna or 'Sorcerer Tree' was next. It was a wide, white-barked tree with hundreds of arm-like branches and spiky, razor-sharp leaves. *La Lupuna* earned its reputation for sorcery because, people claimed, any intruders with an evil heart who ventured near it were attacked by one of its branches.

El Árbol de los Dioses or 'Tree of the Gods' was at the bottom of the page. Someone had drawn a circle around it in purple ink.

El Árbol de los Dioses

Legends say that *el Árbol de los Dioses* was a tree of magic which once bore the world's most extraordinary fruit. Covered in a scaly green skin poisonous to the touch, the berry took over five years to ripen. Underneath this skin was a bitter-sweet pulp which granted godlike powers to whoever ate of it. The juice of this fruit was drunk in a sacred ceremonial rite whenever a new king was crowned, and cultivated by shamans in the cloud forests surrounding the Temple of the Sun. In 1520, terrible blight destroyed many crops throughout Peru including, some historians claim, all *los Árboles de los Dioses*. Twelve years later, Europeans arrived, bringing war and smallpox with them. Shortly afterwards, the reign of the Inca empire came to an end. Conquistadors burnt down the sacred gardens adjoining the Temple of the Sun and *el Árbol de los Dioses* was never seen again.

Underneath this paragraph, at the bottom of the page, there was a handwritten note. It said:

Darling,
I haven't much time.
There was enough juice to fill ten capsules.
You will find them inside the mints. Remember,
this potion is extremely powerful and unpredictable.
Do NOT take more than one. It modifies genetic
coding in ways no one can foresee.
I must rush back before Ricardo notices I'm missing.
Destroy the handbook after you've read this.
Until we meet in London.
Forever yours,
Sx

'Looks like you were right about the second sweet,' I said. 'Thanks for the warning.'

Sadie didn't answer me. Eyes wide with excitement, she leapt to her feet. Aidan!' she cried. 'Don't you know what this means?

'No!' I said, energised by her enthusiasm and hopping out of my seat. 'What does it mean?'

'Your parcel *was* top secret,' Sadie said. 'Those

weren't gobstoppers inside the mints. They were capsules. You and I have drunk from the Tree of the Gods!'

As if in reply, smoke curled out of my ears and sparks flew from my fingertips.

It had to be true!

What else but the Tree of the Gods could have given us these strange powers? We spent the next hour talking about what we should do. Contacting Hussein was step one, though that didn't prove easy. He wasn't returning our calls or texts, which meant he was probably practising his electric guitar and wouldn't get back to us until tomorrow.

Step two was our parents. What should we tell them? In the end, we agreed to keep our abilities a secret for now. There was no need to worry our mums or Mimi, Sadie's older stepsister. Besides, we might wake up tomorrow and find ourselves back to normal.

But for now, we needed some answers, and that was step three. Sadie and I made a list of what needed to be done, arranged it in order and divvied up who should do what.

A To-do List, as agreed by S. Laurel-Hewitt and A. Sweeney in the aftermath of recent extraordinary events:

Sadie	Aidan
1. Read the *Cambio Laboratories* booklet. Determine whether it offers any clues to the origins, consequences and possible side-effects of *el Árbol de los Dioses*	1. Hide the jar of Nature's Own in an old shoe
2. Investigate the origins of *Cambio Laboratories*. Do they rely entirely on proceeds from Nature's Own to sustain their research?	2. Do not – repeat, do NOT – 'surprise' Granny by burning her slippers, walking stick, robes, etc. when she isn't looking

3. Research Ricardo Sanchez, the lead scientist at *Cambio Laboratories*. Explore his work, publications and research interests. Is he 'S'?	3. Do not – repeat, do NOT – burn down Caversham School or 'surprise' classmates and teachers by lighting desks, schoolbooks, lunch trays, etc. on fire when no one is looking
4. Look into the biochemistry behind *el Árbol de los Dioses*. Can a serum possibly explain such immediate, transformative changes?	4. Corner Hussein at school. Discover whether he has also developed new powers
5. Experiment with new skills	5. Experiment with new skills under agreed safety conditions (e.g. whilst a fire extinguisher, bucket of water or Sadie are present)

'Teamwork,' I said, initiating our secret handshake (three back hand-palms, two hand slaps, up fist-bump, down fist-bump, up fist-bump, down fist-bump, three bumblebee wiggles and a waving woggle to finish).

'Teamwork,' Sadie grinned.

MUM

The elevator pinged. Footsteps padded across the landing. A handbag opened. Keys jingled and the latch clicked.

Mum was home.

I met her at the door. 'Mum!'

'Aidan.' She dropped her bag and threw her arms around me. 'Sorry I'm so late. Have you eaten?'

'Yes.'

'Good. And Granny? Is she in?'

'No. She's down the pub, and with any luck, she might not come home at all.'

'Aidan!' Mum said. Pulling me closer, she whispered into my ear, 'Not so loud.' I picked up her bag and, arm-in-arm, we walked into the kitchen. Lemon appeared, her tail twitching.

Between spoonfuls of tomato soup, Mum told

me about her day, from an ailing old man with a bad hip who needed a lift in the ambulance, to the little girl who stuck a marble up her nose and called 999. By the time she finished, her yawns had lengthened. Her head drooped.

Mum pushed her chair away from the table. 'You wait here. I just want to get out of my work clothes.'

While she changed, I took a saucepan out of the cupboard and placed it on the stove-top. I poured a mug of milk into the pan and then gently stirred in two heaped spoons of cocoa, and waited for it to steam. When it was ready, I poured it into Mum's favourite mug, the one with a photo of a five-year-old me plastered on to its side.

I crept slowly down the hall so as not to spill the cocoa. When I reached her bedroom door, I stuck my head in and called out, 'Surprise!'

There was no answer.

Curled up on the bed in a T-shirt and jammie bottoms, Mum was fast asleep.

Four phrases (in no particular order) that best describe Mum, aka Emma Sweeney, aged thirty-five:

- Fair-haired, brown-eyed, slim, fond of tulips, green tea and shoe shops
- Paramedic with the London Ambulance Service, keen cyclist and vegetarian
- Collector of stones, occasional swimmer, karaoke enthusiast
- The best

I left the mug of cocoa on the chest of drawers. If Mum woke up in the middle of the night, it would be waiting where she couldn't miss it. On the way out, I stopped in front of the photo of Dad. I picked it up.

Dad.

He looked smart in his Army uniform – khaki jacket buttoned up, tie knotted, red-rimmed cap on, three shiny medals pinned across his chest.

Lance Corporal Seamus Sweeney.

I was nine when he died. My dad survived three tours abroad. Gun-shots. Bomb blasts. Snipers. And what got him in the end? An accident on the *Autobahn*. A lorry hit a patch of ice and overturned two years ago in Germany, taking two Army vehicles with it. Dad was in the second one.

Dad was never around much when I was growing up. When he did come home for Christmas or birthdays, he always seemed eager to get away again. Not that I'm complaining. I have Mum to look after me. I have Lemon. I have friends like Sadie and Hussein. That's more than most.

I put Dad's photo back on the table.

After retracing my steps to the kitchen, I tidied away the saucepan. I cleaned Lemon's litter tray and put fresh water into her bowl. Beside the bowl, I left a Kit-o-licious treat for the morning.

I unfolded the camp-bed in the sitting room and got my duvet out of the closet. From under the sofa, I pulled out a suitcase – my makeshift wardrobe now that Granny had laid claim to my room – and changed into my PJs. I turned off the lights and pulled the duvet up to my chest, leaving my arms and hands free. Though it was dark, I could make out my fingers in the glow from the street lamps outside.

Whoosh!

Firelight flickered across the ceiling and walls.

When I waved my fingers, the flames glimmered, chasing away the shadows in waves of orange and yellow light. If I concentrated, the flames burned brighter, rising towards the ceiling. I found I could even burn one finger at a time, like a sparkler, and shoot fizzes of flame into the air.

Lemon entered the sitting room, padding across the floor and sniffing the sofa. She stopped when she saw the fire.

'Hey, Lemon. Come here, girl.'

She didn't move.

I turned the flames off, and the room went dark again. 'Come on, Lemon.' I pushed over to make room and patted the space beside me. 'It's time for bed.'

Lemon blinked, but she didn't budge.

Tonight, I was sleeping alone.

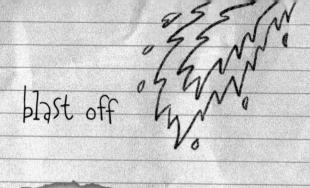

blast off

I checked the hallway and corridor. All was quiet.

'Good. No one is following us.' I opened the gym door for Hussein. 'Come on. This way.'

Hussein plodded in. 'This had better be good.'

Caversham's sports hall was empty and dark. It was morning break, so everyone was outside in the Yard or in form blocks.

After Sadie left yesterday, I tried ringing Hussein again, but it was Extra Maths night which meant two hours at Uncle Ahmad's house and no phone. I'd expected Hussein to race into lesson one to tell me about his new power. When he hadn't, I'd become concerned. It wasn't like Hussein to keep quiet. If I was the Boy with Fiery Hands and Sadie was the Girl Who Made Things Move, what might he have turned into?

'Enough,' Hussein said, coming to a halt. 'This is

weird, even for you. What's so important that we had to sneak in here?'

'I wanted to talk.'

'Talk? About what?'

'About you.' I edged nearer, lowering my voice. 'Are you feeling . . . different?'

Hussein eyed me suspiciously. 'Are you on something?'

This was more like it. I elbowed him in the side and winked. 'Maybe I am. Those sweets yesterday,' I whispered, 'the Nature's Own. Have they . . . *helped*?' I checked the doors to the sports hall. Mitchell Mulch, nosy as ever, had been poking about this morning, shadowing me wherever I went, and I couldn't run the risk of him overhearing. 'Don't worry,' I whispered. 'Your secret's safe with me.'

Hussein nudged his glasses up his nose. His face crinkled as if he were confused. 'Aidan, are you sane?'

I stepped back and glared at him.

'Yeah,' I snapped. 'I am.'

'Then tell me what this is about or I'm out of here.'

Could Hussein *not* know yet?

I pulled him into the centre of the sports hall, where we wouldn't be seen, and rolled up my sleeves. 'Promise me you won't scream.'

Hussein bristled. 'If you're trying to scare me, it won't work.'

'Okay. But don't say I didn't warn you.' I felt a tingle and . . . *whoosh*! My hands burst into flames.

'AAAAAHHHH!' Hussein screamed, stumbling backwards.

Tiny sparks shot from my fingers as my hands blazed orange and red.

Cowering, Hussein put out a hand. 'Are those real?'

'Feel for yourself,' I said.

He edged closer, then jerked his hand back. 'They're hot!'

'I told you it wasn't a trick.' I clapped my palms together and turned the flames off. Hussein came closer and examined my palms.

'There are no marks,' he said.

'I know.'

'No smoke either.' He frowned. 'And you say

this is because of those Nature's Own sweets?'

'Yes.'

He stepped back. 'Do it again.'

I focused on my hands and ... *whoosh*! Ten flames sprang up in place of my fingers.

'That is brilliant!' Hussein said, hopping from foot to foot. He held his own fingers out. 'Show me how to do it!'

I flamed off. 'I don't think I can, Hussein.' I told him about Sadie's powers and the note we had found about the Tree of the Gods. 'You probably have a different power.'

Hussein danced in place, jiggling his hips and pumping his fists. I hadn't seen him this excited since the new *Star Wars* trailer came out.

'What do you think mine might be?' he cried.

'You'd make a great Hulk,' I said. 'I can see you ten times bigger and all green, smashing buildings as you walk along.'

'Really?'

'Definitely. Or Iron Man, shooting through the sky, kitted out in red and gold.'

'I'd need a robotic suit for Iron Man.'

'True. How about being super-fast like the Flash?

Here one second, gone the next.'

Hussein giggled, then blushed. 'Maybe I'll be irresistible to girls.'

I held up a hand. 'Let's not get carried away. Superpowers can only do so much.'

'I guess you're right,' he said.

'You know I am. Trust me, these powers are dangerous. I have to be *so* careful now. It's like I'm on a constant look-out, anticipating danger before it happens.'

Hussein's forehead wrinkled with concern. 'Should there be smoke coming out of your shoes?'

I looked down. There was a small cloud of smoke where I expected my feet to be.

This did not strike me as a positive development. The hands were trouble enough.

Whipping off my shoes and socks, I proceeded to hop, stamp and shake my feet until the smoke stopped.

Hussein watched. 'Has this never happened before?'

'No,' I said, fanning my toes.

'You mean you haven't tried lighting the rest of your body?'

'No!' I snorted. 'Why would I want to do that?'

'Well,' he said, rubbing his chin thoughtfully, 'in terms of physics, we are, of course, in unchartered waters here. Still . . . let's not forget that fire is lighter than air. If you were able to ignite your entire body, you *should* be able to fly.'

FLY?

'Heat rises. Whether you could manoeuvre yourself in mid-air or be dependent on the wind like a kite, I can't say.'

FLY?

'My guess is that you'd have some degree of control. Fire, after all, is a form of energy. Once you learned how to vary the intensity of your own heat, you should be able to take off, turn or accelerate.'

FLY?

I leapt to my feet. 'Stand back, Hussein! I've got to give this a try!'

Hussein backed away as flames licked up my neck and down my back. 'Aidan! No!' he cried. 'Not here! You don't know what will happen!'

Fire crackled across my mouth and nose. 'Commencing ignition!' I shouted.

'Aidan!' Hussein cried. 'Don't! The bell's about to ring!'

My chest tingled. Heat crackled through me, from my arms and legs, from my neck and head. I felt . . . power.

I was no longer a short, ginger-haired, twelve year old.

I was ON FIRE!

Hussein, I noticed, had run off. The heat, I assumed, must have overwhelmed him. I was sorry to see him go. I wanted him to share in my glorious moment of triumph – a human being's first solo flight.

When my feet first left the ground, I trembled . . . but I didn't stop. I wanted more. Clenching my fists and gritting my teeth, I burned brighter.

And it worked.

The hotter I became, the higher I rose. One metre off the ground. Two metres, and rising. Already the world looked different.

I could see the Mr Fitness medicine balls stacked in the back of the storage cupboard.

I could see the layer of dust on top of the climbing frame.

I could see Miss Peyton, our PE teacher, at the door, with a Lower School class queuing up behind her.

Miss Peyton?

Oh no!

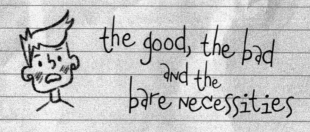

the good, the bad
and the
bare necessities

WHOOSH!

I tumbled to the ground, landing face-first on the sports hall floor as my flames disappeared. As I lay there, I realised two things.

One: though it was hardly a 'flight', I had still managed to defy the laws of gravity – and how many people can say they've done that? Plus, I had learnt an invaluable lesson: ignition was not limited to my hands. I could, if I concentrated, become a boy of fire.

That was the good news.

Two: though I was unharmed, the same was not true of my school uniform. When I ignited, I had managed to burn off every stitch of clothing I had on. Lying there on the sports hall floor, I found myself as naked as the day I was born.

That was the bad news.

the great escape

There was a click. The overhead lights in the sports hall shimmered on and the main door swung open.

Miss Peyton was talking to the Lower School children. 'Find a seat on the floor facing me. We'll do a warm up first and ... holy hockey sticks! Who's that?'

I didn't wait to hear the rest. Scooping up my socks and shoes, I made a bare-bottomed bolt for the exit. This was not a time for explanations; this was a time to RUN! They gave detentions at Caversham if your tie wasn't knotted properly. What would they do if they found me in this state? Lock me away? Force-feed me school dinners? If one of the teachers caught me, I was in BIG trouble.

There was, of course, another – and let's be honest, here – far more important reason for running off.

My peers.

Would my fellow classmates enjoy the story of my naked dash through the school corridors?

Enjoy? They would devour it. They would fall on it like a pack of jackals on wounded prey. They would pick over the bones of my embarrassment with a relish so fierce it would frighten a crocodile back into its swamp. I would never hear the end of it.

So, yes. I ran.

Nipping down the hallway, my shoes and socks strategically positioned at the front and back, I rounded the corner at high speed. Behind me, from the open doors of classrooms, I heard distant cries.

'Did you see that?'

'He isn't wearing any clothes!'

'Hey, you! Come back here!'

I wasn't about to stop. I screeched to a halt at the end of the corridor and opened the door to the Yard, taking cover behind the rough branches of a yew hedge.

So far, so good. No one had recognised me. I considered waiting in the hedge until nightfall, but that didn't seem practical, plus I would still need to walk home. Besides, I had already begun formulating an ingenious plan.

Details of my attempt to preserve dignity at all costs (code-name *The Great Escape*):

1. Manoeuvre around Yard. Avoid detection by clinging to bushes that line the buildings
2. Scoot through canteen. Stay low to the ground
3. Enter D Block through back entrance
4. Find sports bag in changing rooms. Put on games kit
5. Walk to school office with sports bag
6. Claim to have vomited excessively over school shirt and trousers
7. Explain that stinking clothes are now in sports bag
8. Provide further support for story by making loud retching noises in the direction of the school secretary
9. Ask secretary to ring Mum. Request to be collected ASAP

It was a devilishly cunning plan and, if I hadn't

been standing naked in the cold with a yew branch pressed against a delicate part of my anatomy, I would have stopped and congratulated myself. This, however, was no time for a pat on the back.

This was a time for action.

I began the journey around the hedges, stooping low so as not to be seen through the windows or by anyone who might be crossing the Yard. It was a slow, hazardous trek, particularly around the prickly holly bush at the end of C Block, but at last I arrived at the canteen unseen, though shivering and scratched. After first checking through the window in the door and seeing no one, I entered, lowered my head and set off at a trot between the tables. For once, luck was with me. The dinner ladies were busy in the kitchen, so I was in and out of there in no time at all.

That left D Block. I was so close to the boys' changing rooms now, I could smell its fug of musty towels and cheap deodorant. But just as I neared its door, I was forced to turn and high-tail it the other way. Miss Spatchcock, my English teacher, had appeared in the corridor ahead. Forced into a detour, I scampered the other way and nearly ran into Maria Vialli, who, from the sound of her shriek, must have glimpsed my bare buttocks. Hearing footsteps approaching from left and right, I panicked and bundled through the first door I saw. As its lock clicked shut behind me, I turned, uncertain where I was, and found myself staring into the glare of a projector light.

I blinked once, twice, and then realised where I was: on stage in the assembly hall.

Nor was I alone.

Gathered together in rows of chairs were my fellow classmates who, I now remembered, were scheduled to receive a special talk from Mr Henderson, our form tutor, called 'My Body and Me'.

Everyone stopped.

The room hushed.

Fingers pointed, jaws dropped.

There was a huge intake of breath and then . . . bedlam. The hall erupted in barks of laughter, knee-slaps, hoots and howls. Mulch, in the front row, was on the floor, slapping the ground and shrieking.

I held my head high and even attempted a brave smile – not easy with this mob in front of me and nothing but two shoes and a pair of socks between me and my modesty.

It was Mr Henderson who finally came to the rescue. 'Well, Sweeney,' he said, draping his jacket over my shoulders and guiding me offstage, 'it was good of you to offer, but if I'd wanted a volunteer to model this talk, I'd have asked for one.'

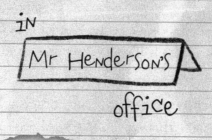

In Mr Henderson's office

D Block was emptied of children. Everyone had been sent on to their next class.

Except me.

I was in Mr Henderson's office. Mr Henderson was behind his desk and Miss Spatchcock sat to my left, an iPad in her hand. She was taking notes. I sat on a metal folding chair in my white sports top and tracksuit, grateful to be wearing clothes again.

Mr Henderson folded his hands over his round belly. 'I think it is safe to say – and do correct me if I am wrong – that your appearance onstage this morning was accidental. Am I right?'

I kept my head down and nodded. Experience had taught me that in situations like this, it was best to say little and look sorry.

'Good. That just leaves the mystery of your

uniform which no one – yourself included – has been able to locate. So tell me, Sweeney. Where are your school clothes?'

'I don't know, sir.'

'You don't know? Are you saying that one minute you're walking about in your shirt and trousers, and the next,' Mr Henderson snapped his fingers, 'they've disappeared?'

This was a tricky one. If I said yes, I made myself out to be a complete numpty, an idiot so clueless he didn't know whether he had clothes on or not when he walked into a room. If I said no, it meant explaining how I lost my uniform. Telling the truth – I burnt it off whilst turning into a human fireball – was not an option.

Numpty it was. 'One minute my uniform was there, sir, and the next . . .'

Sighing, Mr Henderson folded his arms over his chest and stared up at the ceiling.

Miss Spatchcock shifted forward in her seat. 'Aidan,' she said softly, 'it's important we find out exactly what happened.'

I didn't like the sound of that.

'You need to be honest with us. There's no need

to protect anyone. Everything you say in here will be strictly confidential.'

Protect?

'If someone – or a group of boys – took your clothes off you, we need to know.' Miss Spatchcock put her hand on my shoulder. 'That's bullying. Playgrounds can be rough places for young boys like you. You mustn't blame yourself, Aidan. You are the victim here.'

'I am?'

Miss Spatchcock patted my shoulder. 'It's not your fault.'

'It's not?'

Wiping a small tear from one eye, she sniffed. 'No, poor boy. It's not.'

This was news to me. I chanced a smile.

Miss Spatchcock beamed back at me. 'Be strong, Aidan. Be strong.'

I was beginning to warm to her. Unfortunately for me, it was Mr Henderson who was leading the meeting. He returned to the fray, quizzing me for the next ten minutes on where I'd been going, who I'd been with and when it was that my uniform had disappeared.

He wasn't pleased with my answers. 'You're hiding something, Sweeney. That much is clear.'

Miss Spatchcock stopped typing on her iPad and said, 'You can trust us, Aidan. I know you want to.'

I lowered my head and said nothing.

Mr Henderson sighed. Placing his elbows on the desk, he eyed me closely. 'Sweeney, I'm sure you are aware that there is a uniform code here at Caversham, a code which you have broken in quite spectacular fashion – and in my assembly, no less. Normally, I would send you straight to the Head and be done with you. Discipline is his job, not mine. However, I am hesitant to do so in this case.' He gave me a thoughtful look. 'The reason is that a letter that came into my possession recently. A letter that concerns you.'

'Me, sir?'

'Yes,' Mr Henderson said. He opened a thin folder and withdrew two typed pages of A4. 'A letter from your grandmother.'

Uh-oh.

'Do you know anything about it?'

'No.'

Mr Henderson pressed the pages down flat on his desk. 'I didn't think so.' He read through some of it again, frowning slightly. 'Can you guess what it says?'

'I'd prefer not to, sir.'

'It is a permission letter, signed by your grandmother, granting the school the right to punish you by whatever means we see fit. Does that sound like your grandmother?'

'Yes, sir. It does.'

'She seems particularly keen on flogging. There are two paragraphs on that alone.' Mr Henderson put the letter down. 'It says here your grandmother lives with you. Is that so?'

'Yes, sir. She moved in when my dad passed away.'

'I see.' Mr Henderson replaced the letter in its folder. 'Promise me you'll stay out of your grandmother's way, Sweeney. Will you do that for me?'

'I'll do my best, sir.'

Miss Spatchcock reached for the box of tissues on the desk.

'Louise,' Mr Henderson said, 'Would you be

willing to keep a close eye on Sweeney until this matter is settled?'

'Yes,' she honked, wiping her nose.

'Excellent. Sweeney, Miss Spatchcock will act as your personal tutor for the rest of the term. If you have a problem, you are to report to her, and if she arranges a meeting, you are to be there. Understand?'

'Yes, sir.'

And that was that. Mr Henderson even let me go home early.

Result!

I skipped out of Caversham's main doors with a merry heart. The afternoon was mine and now that I could fly, I could go *anywhere*!

Wembley Stadium!

Windsor Castle!

The Buzzsaw – the world's greatest rollercoaster ride!

But then, the reality of flying – of me, Aidan Sweeney soaring through the air like a fiery comet – slowly hit me. Rocketing off into the distance wasn't so simple. Problem one, my clothes. This was all the kit I had left. If I burnt this off . . . well, there was no need to go there again, was there?

Two, I needed flying lessons. Becoming a flaming airplane came without controls, brakes or handlebars. I wasn't sure how to accelerate or slow down. If I didn't want to injure myself or others, I needed to take it slowly.

Three, I was afraid. Rising into the air in a school hall is one thing. Soaring over a city is quite another. Would my flames be extinguished if I flew too high? What if it rained? Would the wind toss me about like a kite? I had plenty of questions, but no answers.

Or parachutes, for that matter.

Until I could find a way to fly safely, I had to keep both feet on the ground – and that meant I had nowhere to go. Home was out of the question. Granny would be there and, given a choice, I'd sooner swim with piranhas than spend my free afternoon with her. There was always the city centre, but I had no money, so what was the point of trooping down there?

In the end, I decided to walk north towards Highgate. Lady Pandora's School for Girls was in that direction, so there was a chance I might run into Sadie riding a pony over the meadow, playing croquet on the lawn, or whatever else the Lady Pandora girls did in their afternoons.

The quickest route to Lady Pandora's was across the Heath, so I entered at its lower slopes and headed north. There was hardly anyone about – a jogger or two, a few dog walkers, a mum pushing a pram. As I rounded a thicket of trees, the path forked. One route led to the bathing ponds and, further on, to Highgate. The other path was overshadowed by a tall, arrow-shaped sign which I had never seen before. It said:

ZARATHUSTRA'S CIRCUS

The World's Greatest Travelling Circus

FOR FOUR WEEKS ONLY
STARTING THIS OCTOBER!

A circus!

Given a choice between visiting a circus or hanging outside a school for posh girls, there was a clear winner. I followed the arrow.

the acrobats

As I descended the hill, Zarathustra's Travelling Circus came into view.

It was ginormous.

A maroon-and-gold striped Big Top towered over the grounds. A flag fluttered from its tall peak and bunting rippled from its sides. Dotted around the circus tent were carnival games, a carousel, funfair rides and food stalls. Two people stood near a shooting gallery stringing light bulbs to its awning and I could hear hammering and sawing coming from inside the Big Top. Outside one of the entrances, a small crowd had gathered.

Clearly, this was worth investigating. I raced forwards for a better look.

A young man and woman in sports kit were spinning through a routine on a gymnastic high bar. Samba music boomed from a speaker as they shimmied in time. A blackboard hung on the fence behind them with a chalk drawing of the woman and man in spangly red tights hanging from a trapeze. Underneath it said: *ESHE* and *RODRIGO*.

Hanging one-handed from the bar, Eshe scissored her long legs into a split and smiled at the crowd.

We clapped.

With her hair cut short and her bronze skin glowing in the midday sun, she looked like an Egyptian queen, a sporty Cleopatra in green trainers. Beside her, Rodrigo matched her movements, shaking his hips and twisting in mid-air as if the sky was his dance floor. A few somersaults, another upside-down pirouette or two and a whirl round the bar and they finished. When they landed on the ground, they each had one hand in the air and the other around each other.

Everyone cheered.

Eshe and Rodrigo bowed. Waving to the small crowd, Rodrigo said, 'Thank you! But no applause, please.' He pointed at the high bar. 'This we use for fun.'

'To train,' Eshe said.

'But a performance ... now *that* is special!'

Rodrigo grinned. 'See the beautiful Eshe fly through the air on the high trapeze!'

Lifting one leg straight over her head, Eshe spun on her toes before leaping into her partner's arms. 'Watch the dashing Rodrigo match her every step,' she said.

Rodrigo spun Eshe into the air. When she landed, Eshe cried, 'Come to Zarathustra's Circus! Eshe and Rodrigo – appearing nightly for four weeks only!'

While the crowd applauded, Eshe and Rodrigo picked up a bag stuffed with circus flyers and began handing them out to the crowd.

'Come to the circus!' Eshe said.

'Fun for all the family!' Rodrigo said, passing out leaflets beside her.

As Eshe worked her way through the crowd, she stopped to chat to two women. A small girl grabbed a fistful of leaflets from the bag while Eshe's back was turned and ran off laughing. Pretending to be cross, Eshe chased after her. This made the little girl chuckle harder and it soon became a game, the two of them darting through the crowd. The girl ended up behind me, peeking out at Eshe from behind my back.

Eshe crouched like a cat, grinning at the girl and prowling towards her.

And then Eshe's eyes met mine.

She stopped.

Her smile faded.

Eshe pointed a finger at me. 'Rodrigo! It's him!'

'Who, me?' I blubbered, suddenly aware that everyone was staring at me.

Rodrigo bounded forwards. '¡*Que coisa!* You're right!' he cried, his eyes bulging. Kissing the medallion tied round his neck, he blessed himself three times. 'It is as if she magicked him into life!'

'She?' I cried, stumbling backwards.

The crowd seemed to close around me as if trying to prevent my escape.

'But I didn't do anything!' I whined.

And for once, I meant it.

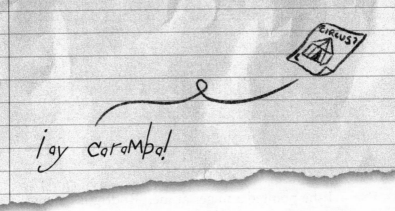

¡ay caramba!

The area near the main entrance was empty. The high bar had been dismantled and carted off. A workman had removed the blackboard and speaker. A few dog walkers lingered near the path, but most of the crowd had drifted off.

Only Eshe and Rodrigo remained behind – and me.

Eshe had recovered quickly. After asking me my name, she'd told the crowd that there was no need to worry. 'Aidan is an old friend,' she'd said. I'd played along, agreeing to stick around until they were alone.

Rodrigo threw a sports bag over his shoulder. 'You surprised us,' he said, leading Eshe and me towards the main gate.

'We've been expecting you for days now. We had almost given up on your coming,' Eshe said.

'You were *expecting* me?'

'Yes!' Rodrigo cried, bouncing on his toes. Unlike Eshe, who glided when she walked, her head high and back straight, Rodrigo leapt about like a puppy after a ball. If he had a tail, it would never stop wagging. 'You know what circus people are like!'

Eshe wrapped her arm around Rodrigo. 'We are not used to new performers joining us, especially one so young.'

Joining us?

'Rodrigo says you are a clown,' Eshe smiled. 'Are you?'

'He must be!' Rodrigo roared. 'Look at his face! How can you not laugh at him?'

'Ha, ha,' I said stiffly. 'You're quite the comedian yourself, Rodrigo.'

Rodrigo laughed harder. 'You see? I told you he was a clown!'

Eshe narrowed her eyes, regarding me coolly. 'I am not convinced. Have you forgotten the fortune-teller's picture? It is Aidan's fire that matters.'

'My f-f-fire?' I stammered. 'What do you mean?'

'You see?' Eshe grinned. 'I hit a nerve. Fire it is then.'

'Fire! How exciting!' Rodrigo whooped. 'I cannot wait to see you perform your act!'

Perform?

'Hold on,' I cried. 'There must be some mistake. I'm not a performer. You must be confusing me with someone else.'

'You are fooling us, yes?' Rodrigo said. 'Playing trick?'

'This is no joke, Rodrigo. I'm no circus star. I'm . . . no one. Even if I wanted to join your circus, I couldn't. My mum would never let me.'

Alarmed, Eshe and Rodrigo turned and spoke swiftly to each other in another language, stopping to occasionally glance in my direction.

I waited.

Finally, Rodrigo approached me. Head down, he threw his arms around me and pulled me into a bear hug. 'Forgive me, amigo, but – *¡ay caramba!* – you should see this picture in our fortune teller's caravan! This boy is your twin!'

'It's true,' Eshe nodded sadly. 'I still cannot believe it is not you.'

Suddenly, Rodrigo's face lit up. 'Let's take Aidan to Dmitri!' he cried. He leapt into the air and grabbed hold of my hands. 'You must come with us to see him!'

'Dmitri?' I asked as Rodrigo tugged me forwards. 'Who's he?'

'Our ringmaster,' Eshe explained. 'You will like him. Everyone likes Dmitri.'

'Dmitri will know what to do!' Rodrigo promised.

I mulled over Rodrigo's offer. Opportunities to meet ringmasters were rare. I also wanted to hear more about my circus double. Could I have an identical twin roaming the circuses of the world looking for work? What did he do? Did crowds whistle and applaud this handsome devil when he walked on-stage?

Was the world ready for TWO Aidan Sweeneys?

I could not leave. Such important questions needed answering. I had to stay and see this through.

Turning to Eshe and Rodrigo, I said with a determined air, 'Take me to your ringmaster.'

whack-a-mole

Inside the circus grounds, men and women were hard at work, hammering in pegs or scrubbing down stalls. Fresh from a hosing, the carousel ponies sparkled and the smells of buttery popcorn and sugary candy-floss wafted over from the food stalls.

Yum!

Maybe I *should* join the circus.

Rodrigo raced off shouting, 'Dmitri! Dmitri! You'll never guess who we've found!'

'He is excited,' Eshe said.

He certainly was. I met Dmitri at the Whack-a-Mole stand. White-haired and thick-chested, he wore a sleeveless T-shirt over old denims. Tufts of white hair sprang from his shoulders and neck and half of one ear was missing. Scars – what looked like claw-marks, mostly – lined both his forearms.

Stubble dotted his chin and his blue eyes opened wide when he saw me.

'This is the boy,' Rodrigo cried.

'Aidan,' Eshe said, 'This is Dmitri.'

The ringmaster grinned. 'Our first visitor in London – and we haven't even opened!' Dmitri chuckled, shaking my hand. 'Rodrigo was right. You are like boy in picture.' When he let go of my hand, he rubbed his fingers. 'And hot-blooded too, eh? I can feel the heat.'

Keen to hear more about my circus twin, I asked Dmitri to tell me more about him and his act. Was this boy an acrobat? A clown?

Incredibly, he didn't know. 'Mathilde speaks in riddles,' he said with a shrug.

'Mathilde?'

'Our fortune-teller,' Dmitri said. 'Mathilde is the one with the picture. It is she who tells us boy is coming.' Scratching the stubble under his chin, the ringmaster eyed me closely as the corners of his mouth curved upwards. 'You should meet her.'

'I should?'

'Yes,' Dmitri said with a wink. 'Mathilde can

answer questions. But not today. She is away. You come back tomorrow. I will take you to her and we will see the circus boy's picture together.' He leaned nearer, beckoning Eshe and Rodrigo closer as well. 'Who knows? If Mathilde is in good mood, she may even read your fortune.'

Rodrigo threw his head back and laughed.

'He has a better chance of finding a gold coin under his pillow,' Eshe said with a smile.

Dmitri's eyes twinkled. 'Mathilde will be good. I promise. So . . . will you return tomorrow?'

Have my fortune told and find out more about this circus boy who was my spitting image? Talk about a no-brainer.

'I'd love to, Dmitri.'

Grinning, Dmitri turned to Eshe and Rodrigo. 'You see? Boys and girls in London want to come to our circus.'

'I am feeling better about England already,' Eshe smiled.

'Me too!' Rodrigo cried.

'Good! And now it is back to business,' Dmitri said, picking up a rubbery-faced mole. Taking a screwdriver out of his pocket, he bent over the

Whack-a-Mole stall and inserted the mole head into its hole. 'I am returning Mr Mole Number Three to his home,' Dmitri said. 'He has become shy and needs more spring in his step. A mole who will not pop up will not do.'

'I love Whack-a-Mole,' I said.

'Me too,' Dmitri said over his shoulder. 'Problem-solving with mallet. Good for soul.'

We watched him reattach the mole head to its spring with pliers and a screwdriver. When he finished, Dmitri flicked on a switch and the stand lit up. 'Shall we see if it's working?'

'Yes, please!' I shouted.

We had three goes each. Eshe and I tied for second – twenty-one each. Rodrigo came last with seven – he just banged everything – and Dmitri was way out in front with fifty-three. Those moles didn't stand a chance against him. The man was magic with a mallet.

'How did you get so good?' I asked him.

'We know each other long time. I take Whack-a-Mole apart. I put together. Many times. Moles pop out in order. Mole five, mole two, mole one, mole three . . . you see? Moles repeat, repeat, repeat. No surprises.' He nudged me gently and smiled. 'Not like people, eh?'

Twenty whacked moles and you won a prize. Dmitri said he owed me and Eshe each a stuffed bear.

'Bears are still in boxes,' Dmitri said. 'When you come tomorrow, I give you prize. Who knows,' he winked. 'Maybe circus boy will show up too.'

fancy that

Little sparks buzzed from my arms and legs as I walked home. So much had happened today! Lost in my own thoughts, I didn't look properly when I stepped out into the street.

Tyres screeched and a taxi slammed to a stop in front of me.

'Oi!' the driver shouted out of his window. 'Watch where you're going!'

Head down, I nipped across to the other side as his horn blared. 'Bloody kids!' the driver roared, as he pulled away. 'You think you own the road!'

On the corner, two girls in Caversham blazers giggled. One shouted, 'You shouldn't complain! At least he has his clothes on!'

Oh, fudge.

Meeting Eshe, Rodrigo and Dmitri had banished thoughts of this morning's assembly from my head.

It seemed no one else had forgotten though, or would for quite some time. A quick and hasty retreat was what I needed, so I scurried past the boys and girls in Caversham uniforms gathered outside of Bartek's Food with my head down. With any luck, no one else would notice me.

Unfortunately, someone did.

'Sweeney!' Mitchell Mulch roared. 'I didn't recognise you with your clothes on!'

Mulch.

Just my luck.

Four phrases (in no particular order) that best describe Mitchell Mulch, aged twelve:

- Short, sandy-haired, big-eared, and – for reasons that defy logic – considered 'cute' by girls our own age
- Only child of Marcus Mulch, property tycoon, and Dr Vanessa Mulligan, dentist
- Attention-seeking, fond of pranks and loud behaviour, occasionally quick-witted
- A royal pain in the you-know-where

Mulch shuffled forwards like a freckly

bloodhound, snorting and yapping. His big ears flapped in the wind. His beady eyes gleamed.

'*What* were you thinking?' he cried.

A crowd gathered round as Mulch circled me, slapping his thigh and laughing as I pondered the consequences of hurling fire at his feet.

Joe Jackson elbowed his way through the crowd, a Slurpee in one hand and a jumbo-sized bag of corn frizzles in the other. 'Sweeney,' he said, tossing the packet of crisps to Mulch. 'I didn't think you'd show your face so soon.'

'And why not?' Mulch barked. 'He's shown us everything else!'

A few boys laughed. I gave Mulch a cold, defiant look.

'You do know they filmed today's assembly?' Mulch said.

My steely mask crumbled. 'They did?'

'Henderson was videoing it. Said he wanted to use his talk as a teaching tool! Good luck with that!' Mulch hooted. 'Won't be long before someone nabs a copy and posts it on the internet.'

This suggestion met with roars of approval. Someone shouted, 'Do you know what they're going to call it? *Pants and How to Lose Them*!'

'I've got a better one,' someone yelled. '*Grin and Bare It*!'

This brought more cheers.

'No, no, no, no!' Mulch said. 'It has to be . . . *Ginger Nuts: The Movie*!'

Everyone fell about laughing.

Ho, ho, ho.

I laughed with them. I had to. There was no escaping this. Sulking would only make it worse.

Coming up for air after a long swig from his Slurpee, Jackson said, 'Don't know why you lot are laughing. Fair dues to Sweeney, I say. It takes guts to show off *that* body.'

Mulch wiped a tear of laughter off his fat cheek. 'Yeah, Sweeney, I have to thank you. That was *the* best assembly ever.' Opening the jumbo packet of crisps, he held it out to me. 'Want some?'

'No, thanks.'

I knew better. This was a trick. Either the bag was booby-trapped, or Mulch would snatch it away as soon as I put my hand out.

'C'mon, Sweeney,' he said. 'Go on. Try some. They're hot and spicy, just the way you like them.'

My fondness for spicy foods – and really, what couldn't be improved by Tabasco sauce? – was well-known. 'How hot?' I asked.

'Red-hot and smothered in chilli pepper. Flame-grilled too.' He rattled the packet of corn frizzles in front of me. 'Go on, try one.'

Flame-grilled? Now that was an idea.

'Maybe I will.' I reached into the bag.

Mulch, oh-so predictably, snapped the bag shut before my hand could touch the crisps and whipped it away. 'Loser!' he sniggered. 'When will you learn?'

I didn't answer him. I didn't need to. His bag of corn frizzles exploded a second later.

BANG!

It seems if you flick fire into a packet of Red-Hot Chilli-Flavoured Flame-Grilled Corn Frizzles and then seal the bag, it goes off like a firecracker.

Fancy that.

FLAME ON!

Sadie and Hussein were in the lobby of our apartment block when I got home. Hussein sat in a battered armchair gaming away on his phone and Sadie stood bouncing a tennis ball off the floor. Or at least, that's what I thought she was doing. When I got closer, I noticed the bouncing ball never hit the ground.

'Never fear. Sweeney is here,' I said, strutting across the lobby floor. 'You'll never guess where I spent my afternoon.'

The tennis ball stopped in mid-air and hovered there. 'The library?'

'A detention cell?' Hussein said.

'Wrong and wrong again. I've been backstage at the circus.' Hopping on to the arm of the chair, I told them about the last few hours.

'How bizarre,' Sadie said when I had finished.

'A circus boy who looks like you! I wonder what he does.'

'I bet he's a human cannonball,' Hussein said, nudging his glasses up his nose. 'Not only could a kid curl up tight into a ball, he'd travel further than a grown-up when you blasted him out of a cannon.'

Hopping off the chair, I boogied forward, cutting up the lobby floor with my best disco moves. 'We can be sure of one thing,' I said, swivelling my hips. 'If he looks like me, he must be a hit with the ladies.'

'Is that with his clothes on or without?' Sadie smirked. 'Hussein told me about your assembly.'

I stopped swivelling and glared at Hussein. 'I bet he did.'

Hussein laughed. 'Mate, you've pulled some howlers in your day, but that was one for the record books.'

'I'm glad you found it so funny,' I snapped.

'I did try to warn you,' Hussein chuckled. 'What happened with Mr Henderson? People are saying you got suspended.'

'Me? No way. They think I'm the victim.'

'You?' Hussein gasped.

'I guess they figured no one in their right mind

would walk into an assembly with no clothes on unless they were forced to.'

Sadie began to giggle. Hussein joined in and was soon laughing so hard he shook.

I was less amused. In fact, I was very tempted to swat them both over the head. Fumes of smoke poured from my collar and sleeves. 'Think it's funny, don't you?'

'Yes!' they cried.

Drying his eyes, Hussein pulled an old rolled-up comic book from the pocket of his hoodie. 'Here,' he said. 'You might find this helpful.'

It was a copy of *The Fantastic Four*. On its cover the Human Torch was zooming up into the air. Behind him, a trail of yellow flames flickered, stretching down to the city far below him. A word balloon said, 'FLAME ON!'

'There might be some tips in there on how to fly,' Hussein said.

I opened it. On the first page, Johnny Storm (aka the Human Torch) floated in mid-air, ember-red against a clear blue sky. Though he blazed and burned, you could still make out his features, his thick chest, his muscular arms. Yellow flames surrounded him, flickering along the length of his body.

'Did I look like that?'

Hussein studied the picture. 'Sort of. More yellowy though, not so red.'

'Thanks.' I rolled up the comic to read later. 'So, what about you, Hussein? You must know by now if you have a power or not.'

'I do.' Hussein's eyes glittered and his brown cheeks glowed.

'Wait till you hear this,' Sadie grinned. 'It's perfect.'

'I can control *machines*,' Hussein said with delight. 'Computers, phones, alarm clocks – you name it!'

'Hussein! That is so cool! You couldn't have chosen a better power!'

Hussein beamed. 'I know. *Computers*!'

'Think of what you can do with an Xbox! You'll be a legend. People will pay to watch you play *FIFA*!'

He hopped out of the chair and practically danced around me. 'I know! I know!'

'How did you discover it?'

'By accident. We piled into the ICT suite after

lunch today and, as soon as I sat down, I knew something was different. Once I touched the keyboard, it was as if the computer was talking to me, asking me what I wanted to do. The columns of numbers that scrolled past when I rebooted made sense. It was as if the computer and I were on the same wavelength.'

'That's amazing!'

He flashed his phone at me. A long-eared goblin in a robe snarled back, waving his lightsabre around. 'I've reached level 89 of *Jedi Academy VI* already. The best I ever did before was achieve Apprentice status. This is . . . incredible! It's unheard of, record-breaking!' His eyes widened. His voice cracked with emotion. 'I'm making history.'

Sadie patted him on his hood. 'Good for you, Hussein. I'm so pleased for you.'

'What about you?' I asked her. 'Power under control yet?'

Sadie made a warrior pose – arms flexed, jaw straight, legs square – and smiled. 'Oh, yes.' The tennis ball flew from the floor and raced up the wall like a squirrel, carried on across the ceiling, twanged back and forth three times off the furniture and landed in her hand. 'My control is much improved.'

'My turn.'

Never one to be outdone, I made flames shoot from my hair. Sparks burst from my ears. My fingertips glowed and I was about to breathe dragon-fire when Sadie shouted, 'Careful! Someone is coming!'

The lobby door opened.

I doused my flames.

A large, helmet-haired, foul-tempered old woman entered with a giant-sized, Tesco-blue Bag for Life in one hand and a walking stick in the other. Her jowls tightened. Her thin lips twisted. Her squinty eye narrowed and the good one twitched.

'YOU!' she bellowed.

'Granny,' I said. 'You're home.'

life's little pleasures

BoING!!

The old witch stomped across the lobby, her walking stick banging off the floor, her Bag for Life held high like a battering ram. At first, I thought she was planning on slamming me off the back wall, but she surprised me by stopping short.

'Here,' Granny said, dropping the shopping bag at my feet. 'Make yourself useful and take this for me.'

'Will do, Granny.' I grabbed the bag and lifted it – or tried to, I should say. 'Oof! What do you have in here?'

'Life's little pleasures,' she sniffed. 'Cigars, peanuts, cheese and gin.' Her walking stick cut through the air like a sword. 'Break one of those bottles and I'll have your hide.' Ignoring Sadie and Hussein, Granny turned her broad back on them and crossed the lobby to the lift. I shuffled after her, dragging the shopping bag across the floor.

'Hurry up!' Granny yelled at the lift, which was on the 4th floor and descending slowly. '*Cage-Fighter: Armageddon* is on the telly in five minutes and I don't want to miss the start!'

I noticed Sadie and Hussein watching, with wicked smiles on their lips.

What were they up to? It was odd they'd decided to stick around. Hussein avoided Granny like the plague. Even Sadie kept a safe distance when the She-Bear was on the prowl. It wasn't like them to get so close to her.

I didn't need to wait long to find out.

As we stood there, Granny's walking stick suddenly spun out of her hand and hippity-hopped away. The She-Bear stared after it, a thick line furrowing her brow, her fists clenched. 'Did you see that?' she cried.

'See what, Granny?' I asked.

'My stick! My stick! It's hopping about the floor like a mad kangaroo!'

'There's a kangaroo in the lobby?' Hussein asked.

'My stick!' Granny roared, jabbing her finger at

her walking stick which was ricocheting around the room. 'Open your eyes, you fools!'

I said, 'Anyone know what you get if you cross a kangaroo with an elephant?'

The stick zoomed past, nosediving at Granny before pulling up at the last moment.

'No,' Hussein said. 'What?'

Spinning round, the stick turned on Granny and began smacking her on the bottom.

'Giant holes all over Australia,' I said.

'Help! Help!' Granny cried. 'My walking stick is possessed!'

A bell pinged.

As the lift doors rumbled open, the walking stick fell to the floor. I picked it up and handed it to Granny. 'Were you looking for this?'

She snatched it out of my hand. 'Give me that!' she growled, gripping it tightly with both paws. 'And don't forget my bag.'

I dragged her Bag for Life into the lift. Sadie and Hussein got in too and stood beside me.

'Sadie,' I whispered. 'That was brilliant.'

'I haven't forgotten the time her stick "accidentally" landed on the back of my shins,' she said with a grin.

'Or the time she "nudged" me down the steps,' Hussein said, rubbing his hands together. The doors to the lift slammed shut. 'Hold on to your seat belts. It's my turn now.'

I found myself gripping the safety bar. We ascended slowly, before stuttering to a stop. The lights shimmered and went out, leaving us in total darkness. From Granny's corner of the lift there came a thump. 'Start working, you miserable box of bolts!'

The lights blinked back on. The motor revved.

'You see?' Granny chortled. 'You just have to show a machine who's the boss and—'

BOOM!

The lift snapped forward, whizzing us up to the seventh floor like we'd been blown out of cannon and then – BOOM! – hurtling us back to the basement. Faster than any thrill ride, speedier than any roller coaster, we boomeranged up and down. Hussein, Sadie and I whooped and screamed. My legs bottomed out, leaving me clinging to the sidebar to keep from tumbling over. And still, it didn't stop. As soon as we reached the lobby – BOOM! – off we went again, hurtling to the top floor like we'd been shot out of a giant slingshot, the button lights for each floor blinking on and off so fast they could barely keep up.

Granny fell, tumbling head first over the Bag for Life and landing with her bloomers in the air. 'Help! Help!' she screamed. 'The lift's gone bonkers! We're going to die!' The Bag for Life toppled over. Desperate to stop her gin bottles from breaking, Granny threw herself after them, crushing the peanuts and almost knocking us over in the process. 'Make it stop!' she cried. 'Make it stop!'

I would have been happy with a few more spins on Hussein's bungee lift, but he must have felt sorry for the old girl. We slowed down, hovering somewhere between the second and third floors. Hussein straightened his glasses. The lift jolted down, then slowed, shuttered and stopped. Its doors opened.

I hoisted myself upright. 'Oh, is this our floor?'

'Who cares?' Granny croaked, crawling out of the lift on her knees. 'Let me out of here! I think I'm going to be sick!'

We shoved the cigars, gin bottles, cheese and peanuts back inside the Bag for Life. Heaving the bag out of the lift, I waved goodbye. 'We should do this again. It's been a blast.'

'Later, mate,' Hussein said, flashing me a thumbs up.

'Talk soon!' Sadie cried.

The doors to the lift banged shut, and off they zoomed.

sound the alarm

At tea, I told Mum and Granny about the circus, entertaining them with tales of Eshe and Rodrigo's act, my mysterious twin and playing Whack-a-Mole with Dmitri. Finer details like why I was at the circus and not in school, I altered or omitted. Why spoil a good story?

Afterwards, Mum peppered me with questions: How old is Dmitri? What countries do Eshe and Rodrigo come from? Where are the circus performers staying? But it was the mysterious circus boy who intrigued her most. 'I didn't know kids were allowed to perform in the circus,' she said. 'Some acts seem so dangerous.'

Granny lifted one haunch off the side of her chair and broke wind, loudly. 'Circus people are nothing but freaks and thieves.' She pointed her fork at me and grunted. 'You would fit right in.'

'Hilda, that is not amusing.'

'As a matter of fact,' I said, 'I think Granny's right.'

'She is?' Mum blinked.

'I am?' Granny barked.

'I *would* fit in at the circus. Couldn't you see me performing to big crowds in the Big Top, Mum?'

'No!' snorted Granny.

'Definitely,' Mum glowed. 'I think you'd be fabulous. What could you see yourself doing?'

'Do you really want to know?'

'Of course, I do, darling,' Mum smiled.

'You won't get upset?'

Mum was less quick with an answer this time. 'I wouldn't dream of it.'

'Promise?' I asked.

'Promise.'

'I'd like to do something with . . . fire.'

'Fire,' Mum repeated.

'Fire!' Granny cackled, spitting half-chewed grizzle in every direction. 'Sound the alarm! Put the fire brigade on stand-by. This is sure to end in disaster.'

Mum inhaled sharply. 'Do you mean like a fire

officer? Someone who oversees crowd safety at circus events?'

'No, I meant like walking over hot coals in my bare feet.'

'I'd pay to see that,' Granny chuckled.

A lengthy sermon on the evils of fire followed, a lecture which made frequent reference to the burn injuries Mum had witnessed while working with the London Ambulance Service. Fire was a deadly hazard and not to be scoffed at, I was told.

Repeatedly.

I nodded my head obediently.

We had finished tea, so I cleared the table, removing the dishes, cutlery and small mound of chicken bones Granny had piled on her plate. From the counter, Lemon watched, her tail flickering.

Mum turned the tap on. 'By the way, did a delivery man call today?'

Delivery man?

Clenching my buttocks together, I managed to smother a small cloud of smoke before it ballooned out of my bottom.

'No,' I said.

That wasn't a lie. I hadn't seen one *today*.

'Are you expecting something?' I asked.

As I waited for her reply, I told myself to breathe. There was no need to panic. It could be *anything*. Mum had tonnes of stuff delivered, didn't she?

'Yes, from South America,' Mum said. 'A parcel, I believe. Very hush-hush. You're to hand it over as soon as it arrives.'

OK, *now* I could panic. I sank my head on to the kitchen counter, scattering chicken bones.

Mum said, 'I got a call from former Lieutenant Ash Aitkens this morning. It seems he served with your dad. Apparently, he's been trying to get in touch with me all week.

I said nothing.

The ends of Mum's mouth curled into a wide, playful smile. 'Ash tells me he has a secret present for a certain young man.'

A present?

I picked myself off the counter and slid knee-first across the kitchen floor.

YES!

Sweeney scores again!

'There's just one catch,' Mum said.

Uh, oh.

'You can't open it until he gets here.' Picking up a scrubbing brush, Mum plunged the dishes into the washing up bowl. 'He insisted. Under *no* conditions are we to open the parcel until he arrives in London.'

Crumbs.

Now she tells me.

I got a dishcloth out of the drawer and joined Mum at the sink. 'Why would a stranger want to give me a present?'

Mum wrapped a sudsy hand around my shoulder and pulled me closer for a hug. 'He wasn't a stranger to your dad. What he sent you once belonged to your father.'

'*Dad?*'

'Ash said he was going through some old boxes and came across it. Your dad gave it to him years ago and now he thinks you should have it.'

My *dad* wanted me to have the jar of Nature's Own? How could that be?

Mum returned to the washing up. 'Ash was ever so charming on the phone, telling me all about

Peru. That's where he lives now. I'm already looking forward to seeing him when he shows up.'

Granny, however, was unimpressed. 'I wouldn't get your hopes up,' she growled. 'If you ask me, this story stinks.'

'Oh, Hilda,' Mum said. 'Must you always be so suspicious?'

'Someone has to be!' Granny sneered.

'Well,' Mum said, 'you're awfully good at it.'

I'll say.

Granny refilled her gin glass. 'I'm telling you, this Aitkens is up to no good. His story is riddled with deceit.' She tapped her honker. 'You can't get a lie past this nose.'

In fairness, it was hard to sneak a false one past the old witch. I know. I've tried.

'Why don't you believe him?' I asked.

'Simple,' she said, lighting one of her foul cigars. 'If this present is so important, why post it? Why not hand it to you when he gets here? Why post it on when no one's allowed to open it?'

Mum said, 'I did ask him about that.'

'What did he say?'

Mum frowned. 'The line went dead,' she said,

handing me a tray to dry. 'When I tried ringing back, there was no answer.'

'Ha!' Granny jeered. 'You see? That was no coincidence.'

'Are you saying he meant to cut me off?' Mum said.

'Of course he did!' Granny thumped the table with her fist, rattling the glasses and sending Lemon scampering out of the room. 'He's trying to smuggle something nasty into Britain and he's using your son to do it.' A plume of cigar smoke curled out of Granny's nose and mouth. 'When this parcel arrives, I say we burn it.'

'WHAT?' I cried.

'Hilda, be reasonable,' Mum said.

Granny flashed me her crocodile smile. 'Accidents happen, you know. Letters get lost. That's all I'm saying.'

'MUM!'

'I promised Ash Aitkens that we would keep the parcel unopened and safe until he arrived,' Mum said, with steel in her voice. 'Do you understand?'

Granny glared at her.

'I take your silence as a yes,' Mum snapped. She snuck a glance at me out of the corner of her eye. 'And that goes double for you, young man.'

'Me?'

'I know what you're like,' Mum grinned. 'I don't want to hear how this parcel *fell open* or that you unwrapped it by *mistake*.'

I flicked her with the dish towel. 'How dare you?'

A small skirmish ensued. It ended with me in a one-arm shoulder hold-lock and a wash-cloth dangling over my mouth. Those self-defence classes Mum took had a lot to answer for.

'Never raise a towel to your mother again,' Mum laughed. She ruffled my hair as I passed by, and her eyes opened wide in alarm.

'Aidan! Are you all right?' she cried, pressing her palm across my forehead. 'You're burning up.'

'Me? Never better,' I said, slipping away.

Notes before bedtime

Lying on my camp-bed, I opened *Cambio Laboratories: A Handbook* and studied the caption under *el Árbol de los Dioses* once more.

Underneath this skin was a bitter-sweet pulp which granted godlike powers to whoever ate of it.

I didn't feel like a god.

Moving slowly so as not to wake Lemon, I tossed the handbook into my suitcase and stared up at the ceiling. Four issues were troubling me.

1. **Fireproof pants**

   I checked online – no one stocks fireproof pants, not even Asda. A firefighter's kit wouldn't do either. The temperatures I generate when I ignite would shred a firefighter's trousers in minutes. Nuclear power plants don't have jumble sales, do they?

2. Flying lessons

Flying while on fire does not, as far as I know, come with an instructional manual. This means I will need to learn how to fly myself. Beginning with a straight up and down seems the best option. Turns I can leave for lesson two. Should I use the roof of our apartment block as a launch pad?

3. The circus

I feel a strange pull to the circus, almost as if Zarathustra's Travelling Circus is calling me. Why? Do I harbour a secret desire to walk a tightrope? Do I fancy life as a clown? Or is it this circus boy summoning me? Might we *really* be twins?

The last item on my list I drew: a box wrapped in brown paper with the word DAD written on top, lines jutting out from it as if it were glowing.

Dad.

Otherwise known as Lance Corporal Seamus Sweeney.

He couldn't possibly be the same S who wrote the note in the Cambio handbook.

Could he?

project mayhem

Mum wasn't back from her night shift when I left for school the next day, so I left her a note on her bedside table.

Sweet dreams,
Mum!
See you soon,
Ax

Granny was midway through her morning routine – a poke at the pigeons gathered outside her window, a fry-up and a spot of dumb-bell curls – so was best not disturbed, which was fine by me.

Hussein and I arrived at Caversham to great fanfare. Herds of second and third-formers bellowed as I walked by, some urging me to keep my kit on, others howling at me to take it off.

I sauntered up the school steps. 'Make up your minds, will you?' I shouted. 'Clothes on? Clothes off? I haven't got all day!'

That got the rabble going. But just then Miss Spatchcock showed up. Silencing the yobs at the gates, she led me through the near-empty hallway to her classroom.

Head lowered, I took my seat obediently.

'So,' she said, perched on the corner of her desk and eying me curiously. 'How *are* you?'

Anticipating this line of questioning, I decided to play on Miss Spatchcock's sympathy. I stared forlornly at a spot on the floor and sighed. 'OK, I guess.'

'You don't look very well.'

I heaved another sigh. My chin trembled. I rubbed my eye as if brushing back a tear.

'Maybe you've come back too soon.'

'You mean I can go home?' I asked, brightening.

'No.' Miss Spatchcock blinked pleasantly at me from behind her large round glasses. 'I'd like to hear about yesterday. You can start with the sports hall and why you were in there. I believe that's where Miss Peyton first saw you.'

It seemed breaking her down might prove more difficult than I had expected. Swiftly changing tactics, I began by apologising for yesterday. I had learnt a valuable lesson, I explained. Arriving fully clothed to assembly had very clear advantages and I promised to observe appropriate dress codes in the future by always checking my shirt was on and my trousers up before entering a classroom. It was, I must say, one of my better performances. I had almost convinced myself that I was sincere. Surely, Miss Spatchcock couldn't say 'No' to that.

I turned to leave.

Miss Spatchcock stopped me.

We weren't finished, it seemed. My 'emotional landscape', she said, needed harvesting.

'My what?'

'Your feelings, Aidan. It's time to give wing to the turmoil of adolescence, to vent the angst of modern masculinity. You need to untie that knot of love and hate inside you and set it free!'

Bloody hell.

It was a bit early in the morning for this.

It took another five minutes of landscape and turmoil talk before I figured out that, basically, Miss Spatchcock wanted me to keep a diary.

'Retain a log of your thoughts and dreams. Chronicle events. Populate pages with the people who inspire and dominate your life. A diary will take you on life's greatest journey, Aidan – the journey into who you really are.'

I cradled my head in my arms and groaned.

'Diaries have enormous advantages,' Miss Spatchcock said. 'Writing will help you overcome life's pitfalls. It will provide a means of communicating your inner worth, a way of turning your shortcomings into strengths.'

'Shortcomings?' I rubbed a knuckle across my forehead. 'Hold on. Are you saying *writing* can make me taller?'

Miss Spatchcock stared at me.

'Biology was never my strongest subject,' I explained.

She handed me a biro. 'Write yourself tall, Aidan,' she said, pointing to the paper on her desk. 'Be the person you want to be.'

Sufficiently motivated, I began beavering away and was still at it when the bell rang. Slouching in for lesson one, my classmates were most startled to see me a) there and b) working.

Joe Jackson gave me a wave. 'Enjoying life on the Naughty Step, Sweeney? I hope Miss isn't working you too hard.'

Mitchell Mulch passed me and sneered. 'They should expel him, if you ask me. The sooner the better.'

'I hate to disappoint you, but Aidan is not serving a detention and he will always be welcomed at Caversham,' Miss Spatchcock said. 'He's here early because he chooses to be.'

Roars of laughter greeted this, my own included.

'Sure he is, Miss!'

'Tell us another one!'

Hussein slid into the seat next to me.

'Ready?' I said quietly.

Hussein rolled one eyebrow up and down. He leered sideways and gave me a sinister chuckle. One day with a superpower and already he had turned into a Bond villain. 'I am very ready.'

On the walk to school this morning, Hussein

and I had discussed how, with the right application of his techno-abilities and my firepower, we could transform the barren wasteland of Caversham School into a wild amusement ride. Working together, we would give the students and staff of Caversham School a day they would never forget! We called this attempted sabotage 'Project Mayhem'.

Incredibly, it worked.

An outline of the intended aims of 'Project Mayhem' and its resulting outcomes:

Aim: Divert computer feed into classroom smartboard so that only *Match of the Day* highlights are broadcast

Status: Achieved

This change of transmission resulted in several stimulating discussions such as which team will win the Premiership title; the merits of VAR (a video assistant referee); and an all-in sing-song featuring our favourite supporters' taunts and chants

Aim: Apply blasts of intense heat to kitchen ovens

Status: Achieved

The toxic blast that followed my visit to the school kitchen at break resulted in the cancellation of the day's planned entrée for lunch (Caversham's notorious cabbage and bean curry). Its replacement – chips, burgers and vegan kebabs from Harvey's chip van – was hailed as a glorious success by children, teachers and kitchen staff alike. Harvey did well out of it too

Aim: Replace school bell that signals the end and start of each lesson with 'The Imperial March' theme music from *Star Wars*

Status: Achieved

This theme music – duh duh duh DUN DA DUN, DUN DA DUN – not only provided much needed amusement to class changeovers, but inspiration as well. Mr Henderson's entrance into Science Lab 3, from his Vader-esque heavy breathing to his 'I find your lack of faith disturbing' line, was spot-on

Aim: Play havoc with the school's heating system

Status: Achieved

Room 9 was rechristened 'the Sauna' during lesson five. Steam poured from its radiators; waves of heat shimmered in the air. The temperature was so high that ink pens burst, the metal coils on ring binders proved too hot to touch and Hussein removed his parka. It was so hot that the styling wax in Mitchell Mulch's hair melted, creating long oil slicks in the aisles. Children lounged across desks, unable to move. School work was suspended

Aim: Shut down the computerised entry codes and registers
Status: Achieved
Shortly after lunch, Caversham School found it could not lock its gates or maintain a register. Once the office discovered it was unable to secure or count the children in its classes, the Head had no choice. Students had to be sent home early for their own safety

The celebrations that greeted the announcement that school was closing were wild and fierce. Children and staff stormed out of the gates in a joyous frenzy.

It was the stuff of dreams.

Hussein and I swaggered after them like two conquering heroes surveying the spoils of battle. Project Mayhem had worked perfectly. We had brought Caversham to its knees. Strolling up the High Street, we plotted more thrills and stunts for tomorrow, each more stupendous than the last.

And then our phones buzzed.

It was Sadie.

A photo of a football pitch appeared. Its scoreboard read:

Highgate: 0 Lady Pandora's: 26

Underneath was the caption: Brazil couldn't stick with Lady P's today!

Our phones buzzed again. This time, up came a photo of a long-haired goalie being hugged by a bunch of girls in purple tops. Goalie was AMAZING. Scored a hat-trick and stopped everything. Two more photos popped up. The first one showed a grinning, wide-eyed girl holding up nine fingers. The second was a selfie of Sadie with whooping teammates behind her and a medal round her neck. On the bottom it said: Cup winners!

26 goals! Hussein texted back. Wonder if Lady P's had help?

Sadie answered with two emojis: a winking face with its tongue out and a smiley face rolling on the floor and laughing.

Bit harsh on Highgate, I typed.

They had it coming, she replied.

We agreed to meet up after tea. Until then, the two Masters of Mayhem had to go their separate ways. I was off to the circus to meet a fortune-teller and Hussein was headed home.

'I'm plugging myself into *Guitar Hero 5* for the rest of the afternoon,' he said, jutting one foot out and strumming the air frantically. 'It's time to put these electric fingers to the test.'

'Good luck with that,' I said, shooting a shower of fireworks over him.

'Best school day *ever*,' Hussein grinned. Sticking his earphones in, he waved goodbye. 'Later, mate.'

I left the High Street and ambled towards the Heath. I was in no hurry because I was early – two afternoons in a row with no school, something I could *definitely* get used to – so I decided to walk past the war memorial outside the Church of the Good Shepherd.

It was nothing showy, just a stone placard on the

outside of church with the names of long-dead soldiers inscribed on it. Not long after my dad died, Mum brought me here to lay a wreath beside it and, ever since, it reminded me of him. Some days, if the street were very quiet, it felt as if I could hear Dad's voice when I walked by.

He never said much, no news from the other side, just questions about ordinary stuff. He'd ask about Mum or school or how Arsenal were getting on. But today was different. This time, one name seemed to ring out across the churchyard: *Ash Aitkens*.

Ash Aitkens!

How could I forget?

Pulling out my phone, I messaged Sadie and Hussein: *Guess what? I know who sent the jar of Nature's Own!* I told them what Mum said about Ash Aitkens and how he knew my dad had wanted me to have the parcel as well as his instructions not to open it before he arrived. After adding that Aitkens would be in London soon, I topped it off with a few dozen fire emojis – my own personal calling card.

And then I carried on towards the circus.

the caravans

Dmitri was standing outside the Big Top when I arrived. He was wearing a long-sleeved red top and held a mug of black tea in one hand. A pair of braces stretched over his thick shoulders, straining to hold up his workman trousers. Stick a few elves in the background and he'd look like Santa on a camping holiday.

I yelled hello.

Dmitri greeted me with a wave and called me over. 'School is finished, eh?' he said, glancing at my Caversham blazer.

'We were let out early,' I grinned.

Dmitri quizzed me about schools in England – what they taught, how large my classes were, what subjects I liked – as he led me towards the rear of the grounds where the circus caravans were parked. Arranged in a circle, they created an enclosure which shielded the performers and their families from visitors.

Dmitri led me into the middle. It was like being surrounded by a ring of wheeled murals. Each caravan was different. One was painted sky blue, another black with gold trim. A leafy green caravan had flowering vines and climbing roses painted on along its sides. Others had phrases in French, Russian or Arabic written across their sides.

'Why are these caravans so different?' I asked.

'We are a travelling people,' Dmitri explained. 'Our caravans are our homes, so each one is different – like us.'

We stopped in front of a sunny caravan with an angel painted across its middle with red wings. Its door opened and Rodrigo bounded out. Eshe swanned down the steps after him, greeting me with a kiss on each cheek.

'Good,' Dmitri said. 'Now we will see Mathilde together.'

We set off, though it was slow going. Along the way, Dmitri kept stopping to introduce me to members of the circus.

A brief list (in no particular order) of the circus stars we met that afternoon:
- Dead-Eye: A tall woman in a long leather jacket and cowboy hat with six guns at her side
- The Red Arrows: A family of Chinese gymnasts led by a man and woman walking on their hands and followed by two girls, three boys and a toddler also attempting (with varying degrees of success) to do the same
- Atlas: A giant strongman with muscles bulging out of his tight T-shirt, who chatted to me as he was working out – if that's what you call lifting a small car over your head
- Kenise 'The Cat' Williams: A woman walking across a rope strung between two caravans
- Various others who were playing a rousing salsa on a mixed selection of drums, fiddles, guitars and trumpets as young children of different ages danced

As we passed by, Eshe swayed to the beat, her arms swinging in time to the rhythm. So did Rodrigo. The music seemed to calm him as he slid gracefully beside Eshe. I kept in step, trying my best to move like them and failing miserably. Not that I minded – it was spellbinding, like stepping foot in another world. I was only sorry Sadie and Hussein weren't here.

Mum too. She'd love this.

At the end of the enclosure, Dmitri stopped in front of a midnight-blue caravan with strange symbols and words painted on its sides.

'Now we see what future holds,' he said.

Rodrigo hopped up and down. Eshe smiled and, behind us, the music stopped and the chatter seemed to hush.

It was time for me to meet Mathilde.

the fortune-teller

Mathilde's caravan was hard to miss. A neon sign with the words 'FORTUNE-TELLER' was attached to its roof.

A list (in no particular order) of the symbols, decorations and drawings painted on Mathilde's caravan:
- A Ferris wheel with a pot of gold at the top and an unhappy king at the bottom
- A child on horseback with sunflowers in her hair
- An upside-down man tied to a tree, with a halo around his head
- A skeleton in black armour riding a white horse and waving a black flag
- Words in what I thought were French and Latin
- The name 'Mathilde' in blood-red letters

And then there was the door.

It had the outline of a hand painted on it, palm facing us as if saying, 'Stop'. In the middle of the hand was an eye staring boldly out, daring those who passed to enter.

I wasn't feeling very daring.

'Dmitri, you're a busy man,' I said. 'I shouldn't be wasting your time. I can always come back another day.'

'I have no plans,' Dmitri said, shrugging.

'Me neither,' Rodrigo said.

'Don't worry about us,' Eshe said, knocking on the door. 'We wouldn't miss this for the world.'

I swallowed, hard. And the door swung open.

What I expected to find inside the fortune teller's caravan:

- A cackling, white-haired, mad-eyed hag staring into a crystal ball
- Jars in a potion cupboard stuffed with wings of bats, toes of lizards, eyes of newts, etc.
- The spirits of long-dead ancestors lingering in corners, eager to chat or recite prophecies of doom

- A black cat who listens in on conversations

What I actually found:
- A teenage girl slouched in an armchair scrolling through her phone

Mathilde's white-blonde hair was shot through with streaks of pink. She wore it long at the front, swept over one eye, and razor-short on the sides. She had two piercings through one eyebrow, one in her nose and an assortment of studs in her ears. Rings covered each finger and leather bracelets looped both wrists. Her denims were torn, her T-shirt ripped and her feet clad in Doc Martins.

Mathilde eyed us sourly when we walked in. She grunted a stroppy greeting at Dmitri and then returned to her phone.

'Mathilde,' Dmitri said. 'We need your help.'

'Zee fortune-teller is now closed,' she said in a thick French accent. 'If you want your cards read—'

'Mathilde . . .'

'Please call back during opening hours. Private sessions are also—'

'Mathilde,' Dmitri said again.

Her sigh was epic – a bone-shaking, shoulder-shuddering, chest-heaving groan that rattled her chair. She placed her phone on the arm of the chair and glared at him.

'Thank you,' Dmitri said sweetly. 'Could we have a reading?'

If her sigh was top class, the eye-roll that followed was magnificent: a delicate fluttering of the eyelids, a spin that swept each corner of the room and a sneer that could have curdled milk to top it off.

It was masterclass stuff, this. I could learn a thing or two from her.

Eshe had a go. 'Mathilde,' she said calmly, 'this is Aidan. Rodrigo and I met him yesterday. We thought he was the boy in your picture, the one you said would join our circus.' She draped her long arm around my shoulder. 'We still think it's him. But Aidan disagrees. What do *you* think?'

Mathilde slid her legs off the arm of the chair. Green eyes narrowing, she studied my face, then my chest and arms. 'Oui,' she nodded. 'Zis is zee boy.'

WHAT?

'I knew it!' Rodrigo laughed, skipping about the room.

Eshe hugged me and Dmitri beamed. 'Welcome to Zarathustra's Circus,' he said.

'I AM NOT A CIRCUS PERFORMER!' I cried.

Mathilde rose off her chair and came nearer. She began circling me, sniffing my arms and legs and staring hard at my arms and neck.

'Is this how she tells fortunes?' I asked Dmitri nervously.

'No,' Mathilde scowled. 'And it is not pleasant. I 'ope I never 'ave to do it again.' Eyes narrowing, she pursed her lips. 'Zere is fire around you. Why?'

'Fire?' I gasped.

'*Oui.* I see flames coming from your 'ead, your chest, your legs. Zis, I do not understand. 'Ow can it be?'

I staggered backwards. 'I don't know what she's talking about.'

'Perhaps we should show Aidan the picture,' Eshe suggested. 'That way he can see for himself.'

Mathilde shrugged. 'If you like.'

'This way!' Rodrigo cried, pointing to a curtain at the back of the caravan that I hadn't noticed before. 'Back here is where Mathilde keeps her cards.'

'Cards?'

'Tarot cards,' Mathilde said, arching one eyebrow. 'You know what the tarot is, don't you?'

'Of course!' I snapped, following Rodrigo into the next room. 'I'm not a fool, you know.'

a CONFESSION

I was lying, of course. I had no idea what tarot cards were.

I thought Mathilde had said, 'Tara's cards' – not that I knew who Tara was either, but that's not my point.

I had told a porky to save face, simple as, no further explanation needed.

I knew nothing about the tarot and, even if I had done, I wouldn't have cared. What good were a bunch of picture cards? Nobody could see into the future.

Or at least, that's what I used to think.

Rodrigo pulled back the curtain.

'Here we are,' he cried. 'Mathilde's dream gallery!'

Speechless, that's what I was.

Thunderstruck.

There were no chairs, no tables, no furniture behind the curtain – only framed paintings, some as small as a book, others as tall as a window. Each painting had a name underneath its picture in capital letters.

Mathilde watched me enter her gallery. 'Do you recognise zese people?'

I did.

On the wall in front of me was a painting of Dead-Eye. Sitting on a throne with a rifle in her hand and her cowboy hat for a crown, she was THE QUEEN OF CUPS.

Eshe and Rodrigo were drawn on a high trapeze.

Their painting was called THE LOVERS.

Mathilde was THE HIGH PRIESTESS, done up in Goth make-up and clutching a phone.

THE EMPEROR covered half a wall – Dmitri kitted out in a Russian hat and ringmaster's kit with a whip in one hand and a black bear grinning at his feet.

They were all here – Grandfather Yang, the oldest of the Red Arrows (THE KING OF WANDS), Atlas (STRENGTH), Kenise 'the Cat' Williams (JUSTICE) – and other circus stars whose names I didn't know.

'Did you paint these portraits?' I asked Mathilde.

'Zee newer ones are mine. My mother painted zee rest.' She pointed to the far corner where Dmitri, Eshe and Rodrigo had gathered around a portrait. 'Zat one might interest you.'

'Come!' Rodrigo cried. 'You must see for yourself!'

'It's you, Aidan!' Eshe said.

I strutted over, eager to prove them wrong. And then I saw the picture.

It *was* me!

My hair, my face, my limbs, my clothes – right down to the torn school blazer and ink-stained tie I had on!

That wasn't the half of it though.

In the painting, I stood on the edge of a tall apartment block. Lemon was there too, her paws in the air as if trying to stop me from walking off the ledge. I held Granny's walking stick over one shoulder, the parcel tied to its end. The jar of Nature's Own was in my other hand. Tiny flames licked my face, hands and clothes and I was gazing up at the sky as if I hadn't a care in the world. At the bottom, it said: THE FOOL.

'The Fool?' I asked. 'What's that supposed to mean?'

'I would 'ave thought zat was obvious,' Mathilde snorted.

I rounded on her, eyeing the young fortune-teller suspiciously. 'How did you know about my cat? Or where I live?'

Mathilde shrugged. 'A lucky guess.'

Luck? As if. There could only be one answer.

'Mathilde, are you . . . a witch?'

'No,' Mathilde said. 'My mother . . . little bit. Me? No.'

'Telling fortunes is old art,' Dmitri said. 'Long ago, fortune-tellers sat with kings and queens and warned of wars or droughts. Today, they travel in circuses.'

Dmitri explained that Mathilde told fortunes just as her mother did. People came to her with questions and she gave them answers. But Zarathustra's was different. The circus was home and her roots here ran deep. Before a new performer joined, Mathilde dreamt of them, and then painted them as a tarot card – just as her mother had many years ago.

Eshe said, 'Tell us about the night you dreamt of Aidan.'

'A boy appeared to me as I slept,' Mathilde said. ''Ee 'ad 'air like grated carrot and skin like milk mixed with pepper.'

'Pepper?' Eshe asked.

'Freckles,' I said, pointing at my nose.

Mathilde ambled nearer, her eyes moving from me to her portrait. ''Ee 'ad eyes like raisins and a button nose.'

'Eyes like raisins?' I sniffed. 'What am I, the Gingerbread Man?'

''Ee stood on a 'igh building, a ginger cat at 'is feet. In one 'and was a jar of sweets.' Mathilde watched me out of the corner of her eye. 'Zese sweets were important.'

She swept by me for a better look at the painting. As she brushed past, I caught a whiff of her shampoo.

'It was midday and zee sun was 'igh in zee sky. I could see London in zee distance, its big Eye, zee famous buildings.'

Her hair smelt of coconut.

'In zee dream I say, "Go back. Move away from the ledge", but zee boy, 'ee not listen.'

I like coconut.

'Instead, 'ee burst into flames . . .'

In fact, I never knew coconut could smell so good.

'Zee flames burned, but 'ee did not cry or shout. Zey did not 'urt zee boy. 'Ow can zis be?'

As my head was now somewhere in the tropics, it took a few seconds for this last comment to sink in.

The room fell silent. No one moved. Nothing stirred. Everyone waited for an answer.

What they got instead was a ringtone.

there's no fool like a young fool

'Excuse me,' I said, pulling out my phone.

It was Hussein:

ROOF TERRACE. URGENT. THE DEATH STAR HAS LANDED

Either disaster had struck or Hussein was the last shredder standing in *Guitar Hero*. I stuffed my phone back into my pocket and told Dmitri I had to go.

'Wait!' Rodrigo cried. 'You can't go, Aidan! The circus needs you. *We* need you!'

'Ha, ha. Good one, Rodrigo,' I laughed.

'Rodrigo isn't joking,' Dmitri said. He nodded at the others. 'Could I speak with Aidan alone?'

Eshe and Rodrigo said they'd wait for me outside and left arm-in-arm. Mathilde slouched out through the curtain without so much as a goodbye.

When they left, Dmitri said, 'Our customs must

seem odd to you, eh? Fortune-tellers. Tarot cards. Paintings that foretell the future. They do not teach you about this in England, do they?'

I shook my head. No, they certainly did not.

'Years ago, great crowds queued to see Zarathustra's Travelling Circus. Three times we circled the globe. Three times! Each show sold out. Now … it is a struggle. Times are hard. Crowds no longer come to see us.'

'I'm sorry to hear that, Dmitri.'

The old ringmaster pulled at his collar. His thick shoulders slumped forward.

'London may be our last stop. If my circus cannot fill the Big Top here, we will close. That is why when Mathilde paints, Rodrigo gets excited. Everyone's hopes soar. *A new act will sell seats*, the circus cries. When they see her painting, my people say, *the Fool will save us!*'

'Dmitri,' I cried. 'No one will ever pay to see me!'

'Yes, they will.' Dmitri said gently. 'Maybe not tomorrow or next week, but some day they will. Thousands will come see you one day. Trust me, I know. Mathilde is not the only one who sees the fire in you.'

My mouth fell open.

'It will not be easy. Great trials await you, and many will try to steal your gifts.'

'How can you be so sure?'

Dmitri's craggy face broke into a wide smile. 'In circus, you see many wonders. One day, you will come good.'

I stared up at my portrait. It felt like the word FOOL in its big bold letters was jeering down at me. If this was my future, I couldn't see it ending well.

Standing beside me, Dmitri studied the painting too. To anyone on the outside, we must have looked like an old man and his grandson on a day out at an art museum.

Dmitri said, 'The Fool is very good card. You are lucky boy.'

'If you say so,' I replied.

'It is true. In the tarot, the Fool is a card of new beginnings. It is a hero's card, a call to adventure.'

'Some adventure,' I said, frowning. 'It looks as if I'm about to walk off the roof.'

Dmitri chuckled. 'The Fool is human, like you. Even heroes make mistakes.'

'Tell me about it.' I sighed.

'You are worried, eh? Afraid you might start a fire you cannot put out, a fire that might burn the people you love?'

I nodded my head. So far, I had burnt away one school uniform, scorched my duvet and accidentally set half the bathroom on fire. When I belched, clouds of smoke puffed out of my mouth. When I sneezed, flames came rocketing out of both nostrils. I was a walking, talking fire hazard. It was only a matter of time before I hurt someone.

Dmitri threw his arms out and grinned. 'That is why you should join my circus!'

In the circus, I would learn how to take risks without hurting others, Dmitri explained. Eshe and Rodrigo, Dead-Eye, the Red Arrows – all of his acts – flirted with danger whenever they performed. Working alongside them, I'd discover how they kept safe, instruction I needed if I was ever going to control my own powers. Plus I'd get a tenner a night and all the popcorn I could eat! How could I say no to that?

In return, Zarathustra's would get their 'Fool'.

Ever since Mathilde had painted my portrait, the circus had been cursed by bad luck – Kenise had twisted her ankle; the carousel had broken down; the circus tent had sprung a leak. Circus folk were very superstitious, Dmitri told me. Usually, the circus performers whom Mathilde painted arrived the day she finished her picture. They had waited over a month for me to show up. Until the 'Fool' joined, they believed this bad luck would continue. 'You will bring big smiles to my people's faces if they see you working in Big Top,' Dmitri said. 'They will believe their luck is changing.'

It was a tempting offer. Getting Mum's permission might not be easy, but the job would only be for four weeks while the circus was in town. *And* it would get me away from Granny while Mum was at work.

'I'll do it, Dmitri!' I said.

Dmitri grinned and clapped his hands. 'This is good news! We must tell the others!' Just then, a ferocious *thump* shook the caravan.

BANG! BANG! BANG!

The side door swung open and into Mathilde's gallery strode Atlas, Zarathustra's strongman.

Filling the doorway with his enormous frame, he loomed over me, a balding, muscle-bound giant in overalls and a tight green T-shirt.

'Dmitri,' he grunted. 'We need your help. The rigging on the left entrance has come loose.'

Dmitri stood. 'Go. I will be there shortly. First I must say goodbye to my young friend.'

Atlas swivelled his huge torso so he could see me. His stern features – straight mouth, grim black eyes, severe jaw – softened. His mouth opened wide into a smile of recognition.

'Fool!' he cried. 'You are here at last!'

'You can call me Aidan,' I said. 'It being my name and all.'

Atlas shrugged. 'Fool is better. One word, one name. Like Atlas.' He slapped his thick biceps and flexed his muscles. 'I am Atlas. Strong man, strong name. Like the Titan who held up the sky. And you . . . you are Fool.'

'Yes, well . . .'

'Nikolas,' Dmitri said. 'Go see about the rigging. I will be right there.'

Atlas grunted a goodbye and left, edging sideways out the door.

'I must go after my strongman,' Dmitri said with a wink. 'He pulled the tent down last time and I do not want to spend tomorrow morning putting it up again. Come tomorrow when school is over and we will begin.' Smiling, he shook my hand. 'May your life forever be sweet and your fortunes great. Aidan Sweeney, on behalf of Zarathustra's Travelling Circus, I welcome you to our performing community.'

the roof terrace

Only one family lived on the top floor of Alexandria Apartments – Sadie's.

Her flat was HUGE. It covered the entire floor and came with its own lift, Jacuzzi, three bathrooms, a games room and a wall-to-wall TV. Sadie's bedroom alone was as big as my entire flat and the craziest thing is that she was hardly there. As soon as school broke up, Sadie was out the door: skiing in the Alps, scuba-diving off the coast of Australia or on safari in Africa. There wasn't a continent in the world she hadn't visited.

Sadie's mum was rarely there either. She was an actor called Alice Laurel and she spent most of the year in America filming *The River*, a Netflix series which I wasn't allowed to watch. It was *The River* that paid for Sadie's flat.

Sadie's stepsister, Mimi, looked after her whenever Sadie's mum was away. Mimi was in her mid-twenties and good fun, the kind of adult who wasn't really bothered what you did, as long as the neighbours didn't complain and you didn't wreck the place.

Mimi was a costume designer at Landmark Films. That meant fancy-dress parties, Halloween and red-carpet events were taken very seriously in the Laurel-Hewitt household – we're talking months of preparations. Show up at one of their costume parties in a paper mask and they might send you packing.

Really? That sounds like an exaggeration.
It's not.

Let me decide that. Tell us more.
A young boy once showed up at Sadie's fancy dress birthday party sporting a 'Honey Nut Monkey' mask, a cardboard face he had cut out of a cereal box. Mimi did not approve. 'You could have at least made an effort,' she told him.

Did the young party-goer take this criticism on the chin?

No, he did not. He tore his 'Honey Nut Monkey' mask into a million pieces and stomped home, howling loudly. There he stayed, weeping bitterly until Sadie arrived with a large slice of chocolate fudge cake. Being the truest of friends, she chose to forsake her own birthday party upstairs (she was seven) for him, and they spent the rest of the afternoon happily making Lego castles.

Did he learn his lesson?

He most certainly did! His most recent costume – a daring makeover as Pippi Longstocking for New Year's Eve – received plaudits from Mimi herself and many others, some of whom, like Mimi, worked in the fashion trade.

At the door, I tucked my shirt in and licked back my hair – just to be safe. Suitably attired, I pressed the doorbell.

Mimi opened the door, her headphones on and music blasting.

'Thanks, Mims.'

Mimi smiled at me as I came through. 'She's on the roof!'

I darted into the lounge, where the sliding doors opened out into a roof garden. The view was brilliant from up there – St Paul's and the Gherkin in front, Highbury and the Emirates behind, the hills of Highgate and Hampstead to the west and Canary Wharf to the east. It was like sitting on a London mountain top.

I found Sadie and Hussein in the roof garden, sitting at a table, huddled around a laptop. Hussein seemed jittery, tugging on the collar of the shirt and biting his fingernails.

Nothing unusual there.

Sadie had her puzzle-face on – mouth pursed, eyebrows pinched, hair pulled back tight – and did not look like she wanted to be disturbed.

Oh, well.

'What's up?' I said, sliding into a seat next to them. 'You two look as if a cat weed into your cornflakes.'

Interesting fact:
Lemon once did this to my bowl of Cheerios. Mum

165

said Lemon was 'marking her territory'. I said it was 'revenge for not sharing the last of the milk'. I wanted to give the Lemony Cheerios to Granny – purely as a science experiment – but the smell was too revolting and we had to bin them.

'It's about time you showed up,' Hussein said.

'Good to see you too, mate.' I turned to Sadie. 'Is something wrong?'

'Our lives are in danger,' Hussein snapped. 'Is that wrong enough for you?'

Typical Hussein, always exaggerating. I was halfway through a decent imitation of Mathilde's eye-roll when Sadie stopped me.

'He's not joking, Aidan. It's true.'

'WHAT?'

Sadie took a deep breath. 'Do you remember when we agreed that you would ask Hussein if he had developed a power and I would research Cambio Laboratories and *el Árbol de los Dioses*?'

'Yes.'

'What I found was ... disturbing. I didn't mention it yesterday because I thought it would only alarm you,' Sadie said, twisting the sleeve-ends of her hoodie. 'But I can't keep quiet now. Not if Ash Aitkens is coming.'

My belly flip-flopped – and not in a good way. It felt as if a hole had opened up in the roof terrace and I had fallen through it.

'Brace yourself,' Hussein said darkly. 'You're not going to like what you're about to see.'

On the laptop screen, a headline scrolled past:
EXPLOSION ROCKS CAMBIO LABORATORY.

Beneath it was some footage taken from a helicopter at night. Smoke and flames billowed out of a large two-storey building. People, many wearing green tops or white lab coats, stood outside, while firefighters sprayed water into the windows with hoses. When the helicopter flew higher, the many other buildings within the grounds became clearer, lit up by searchlights and the glow of the fire. It was easy to see then why so many fire engines had been called out to the laboratories. Forests as far as the eye could see surrounded the complex.

The video cut to a new scene. It seemed to be the next day. A reporter was standing outside a charred brick building. Behind her, men and women in protective suits moved in and out of a burnt-out doorway. Running across the bottom of the screen was the tag: *Investigators say fire at Cambio Laboratories is 'suspicious'.*

A transcript of Paula Rodriguez's report for 24/7 News:

I am outside of what remains of one of Peru's leading environmental centres, Cambio Laboratories. Yesterday, fire ripped through the main building, cutting down power lines and causing untold damage to equipment and data. Cambio's vast greenhouse, a centre for the cultivation of rare plants, was also destroyed in the blast. For the scientists who worked here, this represents a huge loss. Many of the plants in Cambio's greenhouse and laboratories were one of a kind and irreplaceable.

Ricardo Sanchez, the botanist who heads Cambio Laboratories, is said to be devastated. Sanchez was rushed to hospital yesterday evening where he remains under

observation. Eleven other scientists and
employees were also admitted, one in a
serious condition.

Attention now is being focused on the
origins of the fire – and that's where this
story takes a dark turn. On the day of the
explosion, Cambio Laboratories had
experienced a serious security breach
within its greenhouse. Sources tell me that
the laboratory was in lockdown which meant
that no one was allowed out of the complex
until an investigation had been completed.
When the fire started, the alarm overruled
these restrictions, a detail which
investigators believe is no coincidence.
Police here are convinced that the fire was
started in order to free accomplices inside
of its greenhouse. But what forced Cambio
Laboratories to adopt lockdown procedures
in the first place? Centres for
environmental science do not usually come
with armed guards and fortified fences. What
were Cambio's team of scientists hiding?

The answer to that question, many people

believe, is rooted in legend. Unconfirmed reports claim that Ricardo Sanchez and his team were cultivating the long-lost miracle tree of the Ancient Incans, *el Árbol de los Dioses*. One sip of the bitter juice from its fruit, Inca legends tell us, can give a person godlike powers.

To the modern ear, talk of magic trees and superpowers sounds like a fairy tale, but not in this part of Peru. People in Cambio are convinced this tree exists and that Ricardo Sanchez and staff at Cambio Laboratories were cultivating it in secret. If true, such claims may explain why a team of security guards carried out daily stop and search procedures on employees who entered and exited its grounds.

Did Sanchez and his team locate *el Árbol de los Dioses*? So far, officials have refused to comment. But if the rumours are true, it seems someone was desperate to get their hands on the fruit of this tree – and ready to destroy anyone who stood in their way.

It isn't all bad news for Cambio
Laboratories, however. Younger viewers
may be pleased to hear that Nature's Own,
the sweet factory that operates out of
the grounds, was untouched by the blaze.
Its head of production assures me that it
is business as usual for him and his
workers today. In fact, that rumble you
hear in the background is one of the
Nature's Own delivery trucks heading out
the gates which, if you snack on as many
chocolate peanuts as I do, is reassuring
to hear!

This is Paula Rodrigues reporting *live*
from Cambio Laboratories for 24/7 News.

The video ended.

I leaned back against the bench, struggling to
take in what I had just seen and heard. 'When did
this happen?'

'Five days ago,' Sadie said.

'If the explosion destroyed Cambio's greenhouse,
then that means . . .' I didn't finish.

Sadie placed her hand on my shoulder. 'That

means those capsules in your jar are all that remains of *el Árbol de los Dioses*.'

My skin turned a vivid crimson, sizzling like a hamburger on the grill. It was no use. I couldn't keep the fires raging inside me any longer. 'You may want to avert your eyes,' I said, pulling my top off over my head.

Backing away, Sadie's mouth fell open.

Hussein slammed the laptop shut before the heat shimmering off me melted the screen.

Hopping out of my seat, I kicked off my trainers as I tried to undo my trousers. 'I feel an explosion of my own coming on.'

'Aidan! I swear, if Mimi sees you running around up here with no clothes on—'

I didn't hear the rest.

Whoosh!

Bursting into flames, I rose into the night sky.

real flying

If you ask me, Superman has a lot to answer for.

Watch him and you'll see what I mean. One arm pointed at the sky, he stands on a rooftop, his feet square, red cape rippling backwards in the wind. His hair is perfect. And then . . . lift off. No bending of knees, no flapping of arms. He doesn't even lean forward. *Zoom!* Off he soars. Up, up and away.

Rubbish, that is. A cartoon. Make-believe.

Real flying is far more complicated.

Just as I did in the sports hall, I initially rose only a few feet into the air. I physically couldn't go any higher and, to be honest, I was afraid to try. The wind was blowing mighty hard above Alexandria Apartments, which made it hard to control where I was going. Between the chimneys and rusting aerials scattered about – not to mention the flock of squawking pigeons who flew off in a flap after I came blazing by – the rooftop was one big obstacle course.

I soon made an important discovery, however. When I burned hotter, I rose higher into the air and flew faster. This meant that as long as I was red-hot I could fly into the wind. Admittedly, I was still learning how to vary my temperatures, so there were a lot of stops and starts, but I eventually managed to fly back to Sadie and Hussein. I crash-landed near the roof garden, tumbling to a halt, my flames out.

Were my two friends worried?

Were Sadie and Hussein relieved to see me back on the roof, safe and sound?

Not exactly.

'GET YOUR CLOTHES ON!' Sadie cried, a hand over her eyes.

'And stop messing about!' Hussein added for good measure.

Like I said, Superman has a lot to answer for.

Snakes and ladders

A tall jug of water sat on the table. At my side were a fire blanket, a bucket of ice and a slim fire extinguisher.

'You're not taking any chances, are you?' I said.

Sadie shook her head. 'We can't. Not now. We haven't the time. It isn't easy, Aidan, but you must learn to control your power. You can't let it control you.'

She was right.

'I'll try my best. I promise.' I assumed my best deep-thinking expression – forehead wrinkled with weighty musings and arms crossed heavily across my chest. 'So, where were we?'

'Here,' Hussein said, tapping a button on the laptop screen. Up popped a photo of a man in his mid-thirties with a long, straight nose and hazel eyes. His wavy brown hair was parted neatly at the side. He had a dark tan, a cleft chin and smiled at the camera as if it were blowing kisses back at him.

'Never saw him before,' I said.

'Say hello to Ash Aitkens,' Hussein said.

'The same man who sent me the parcel?'

'The same man who plotted the break-in and fire at Cambio,' Sadie said.

'Go on,' I said, pouring the jug of water over my head, just to be safe. 'I'm listening.'

After I'd messaged them about Ash Aitkens, Sadie and Hussein had arranged to meet here and combine forces. Their mission? To solve the mystery of Cambio Laboratories and the *ultra-secreto* parcel.

'I was convinced that the fire and the jar of Nature's Own were connected,' Sadie said. 'I just needed proof. That's where Hussein came in.'

No computer system in the world could withstand Hussein's electro-powers once he was plugged into the internet. Trawling through Ash Aitkens' old texts, emails, bank statements and photos, he found that Sadie had guessed right. Everything – the break-in, the fire, the jar of sweets – originated with Ash Aitkens.

You wouldn't think it to look at him. On the surface, Aitkens looked like a respectable member of his community. He was a former Olympic triallist in gymnastics, had left the Army with an honourable discharge after achieving the rank of lieutenant and was now the managing director of AA Security, a firm with offices in Mexico City and Buenos Aires. He was good-looking, popular and sporty. What more could a man want?

Plenty, it seemed.

'Faster cars, celebrity friends, quick ways to become mega-rich – it's all he ever talked about,' Sadie said.

'Nothing was ever enough,' Hussein said. 'Reading through his texts and emails was like listening to one long moan.'

He stopped complaining when Cambio Laboratories hired him. They paid AA Security an enormous fee to install top-of-the line CCTV cameras, ID scanners, electric fences and more, though he couldn't understand why. Who rigs the finest security money can buy around a *greenhouse*? It didn't make sense. Perhaps this centre for environmental science was more than it seemed. As he was hunting for answers, he discovered one of Ricardo Sanchez's research scientists was English, and decided to pursue her.

'He texted his mates about her from the start,' Hussein said. 'Like it was some kind of game.'

Can you believe it? I've met an ex-pat in this godforsaken part of the world. Her name is Sloane Sixsmith – London-bred, no less – and as miserable and lonely as they come. She may not be much to look at, but just wait and see. A little of the old Aitkens charm and Sloane will soon tell me what Sanchez is hiding inside that greenhouse.

Sadie tapped the screen. 'Here are some photos of the two of them together.'

While Aitkens smiled at any camera pointed at him, Sloane shied away, lowering her chin or turning her back. She was pink-skinned and had lank, mousy-brown hair that fell to her shoulders. In most of the pictures – the ones of the two of them backpacking in the mountains, eating at swanky restaurants and dancing together at a nightclub

– Sloane seemed stiff and awkward. She only seemed at ease in the photos where she was wearing her lab coat or taking leaf cuttings from a forest floor.

'If Aitkens' diary is any guide, he didn't leave her side while he was in Cambio,' Hussein said.

'Why didn't she tell him to back off?' I asked.

Hussein looked at Sadie.

Sadie shrugged. 'She enjoyed the attention, I guess.'

She certainly got enough of it. Aitkens texted her reminders:

Don't forget to take your vitamins before bed!

He left treats for her at work:

A little chocolate each day keeps a smile on your face.

He messaged her advice:

You deserve better, Sloane. Why climb the greasy ladder of success? There are other ways to get what you want.

'A month ago, he seems to have finally got the information he wanted,' Hussein said. 'His texts suddenly became obsessed with the Incas and their sacred orchards.'

'Sloane told Aitkens about the Tree of the Gods?'

'She must have,' Sadie said. 'From then on, he talked about nothing but the wealth and fame these powers would bring – and how to get his hands on them.'

'Aitkens knew how Cambio Laboratories was laid out through his AA Security firm,' Hussein added. 'He had maps of every building as well as their security points, timetables and check-ins highlighted in yellow.' Hussein tapped the keyboard and dozens of emails appeared on screen. 'Read this,' he said. 'It's a reply to his Head of Security, Kurt Schlep.'

Re: Safe route

There's one weak link in Cambio's security chain – the sweet shop. It's perfect. No one X-rays chocolate bars and gumdrops, do they? If we can get the fruit-juice into Nature's Own's post room, we can smuggle it out in one of their boxes. All we'll need to do is slap an address on the box and Cambio will do the rest!

You had to admit – it was clever. I just couldn't understand why Sloane went along with it.

'Isn't it obvious?' Sadie said. 'She did it for *love*.'

I made a face and groaned.

'I know,' Sadie scowled. 'Ridiculous, isn't it?'

'What a waste,' Hussein said with disgust. 'Why would you want to throw your career away for a slimeball like Ash Aitkens?'

'That's not the worst part,' Sadie said. 'One scientist was caught up in the blast and admitted to hospital. Her injuries, doctors said, were "life-changing". This scientist hasn't left her bed since, talking to no one and taking no calls. Guess what her name is?'

'No!'

'Yes,' Sadie said angrily. 'Sloane Sixsmith.'

As the managing director of AA Security, Aitkens knew when and where the security checks took place. Sloane had ten minutes to make the capsules, get them to the Nature's Own post room and return to the greenhouse without being detected. Once she was back Aitkens planned to start a fire that would destroy the Tree of the Gods before the next security check took place. With the entire tree destroyed, no one would know its fruit was ever stolen.

'What happened?' I asked.

'Aitkens didn't set off the explosion until *after* the security checks took place as scheduled.'

'They'd already discovered the fruit had been stolen, the alarms had gone off and the greenhouse had been put into lockdown,' Hussein said in a bleak voice. 'There was no way out after that.'

'That snake double-crossed Sloane,' Sadie said bitterly. 'It was a trap. He started the fire and left her there to die.'

We went quiet.

On the table, the laptop hummed.

Horns blared and sirens wailed in the streets below.

A train cut through the night, rattling north on the overground rails.

Hussein crossed his arms over his chest. 'One more thing, Aidan ... just so you know: Ash Aitkens bought a plane ticket yesterday with his credit card. He arrives in London on Saturday.'

This time, I emptied the entire bucket of ice over my head.

keep calm and
avoid zombies

Night had fallen. Twice Mimi had called us in from the roof, but we remained rooted to the bench, talking over what we should do next.

We came to some big decisions.

We could not let Ash Aitkens leave my flat with the seven remaining jellied mints on Saturday. The last drops of juice from *el Árbol de los Dioses* were far too powerful to hand over to a despicable crook like him. If Aitkens wanted a fight, we'd be ready.

The only fly in the ointment was me. Of all the people in the world he could have chosen, why did Ash Aitkens decide to send his smuggled sweets to me? It was the one mystery Sadie and Hussein hadn't solved.

'We checked three times,' Sadie said. 'Aitkens never mentions you, your mum or your dad by name before the robbery. He talks about a "safe place" and "an address no one will ever trace" and that's it.'

We were certain of one thing, though: when Ash Aitkens arrived in London, he expected to find an unopened parcel.

So we decided to give him one.

Hussein checked online. Littman's Chocolate Emporium kept jars of Nature's Own jellied mints in stock. If we bought a new jar of jellied mints, covered it in Sellotape, wrapped it in brown paper and addressed it to me, it would look exactly like the parcel I had opened three days ago. Aitkens would never know the difference. I even had the original stamps.

Until he opened the jar and tried a sweet, of course.

Then Aitkens would be furious! Robbed of a superpower! Cheated out of fame and fortune!

But Sadie didn't think he would come after me or Mum for nicking the capsules.

'He'll blame Sloane. All Aitkens knows for certain is that something triggered the alarm. He *thinks* she went through with the whole plan, but he doesn't *know*. When he finds there aren't any capsules of fruit-juice inside the sweets, he'll assume she got cold feet after stealing the fruit.'

'Or that she was caught,' Hussein added.

'Either way, he won't suspect you or your mum,' Sadie said. 'He'll probably catch the first plane back to Peru and wait for Sloane to wake up.'

'I still don't understand why we're not telling the police now,' Hussein said, looking worried.

'Two reasons,' Sadie said. 'First, no one will believe us. We are three twelve year olds and Ash Aitkens is a successful businessman who once served in the Army. The police would laugh at us. No one is going to take our word over his.'

This was true.

'Second, we are being watched.'

'WHAT?' I shouted.

'Aitkens sent Kurt Schlep and a team of his security men to London to keep an eye on you and your flat.'

My hair and ears caught fire. 'You said Aitkens never mentioned my name!' I cried, spitting sparks.

The fire extinguisher flew through the air and into Sadie's hand. 'Aidan,' she warned, 'Don't make me use this.'

I took a deep breath and closed my eyes.

The flames disappeared.

'Good boy,' Sadie said, patting my head. The fire extinguisher returned to its place on the terrace. 'As I was saying, he never mentioned your name *before* the robbery. Afterwards though, Aitkens told Kurt and his team to keep a close eye on you, your mum and your friends until he arrived in London.' Sadie smiled at Hussein. 'When that lot are out of our hair and Aitkens is back in South America, we'll post all the files on the internet and let the authorities in Peru handle it. This way no one will ever suspect we were involved.'

Hussein bit his thumb nervously and frowned. 'This is so risky. Do you really think we can fool Aitkens when he shows up?'

'What do you think, Aidan? Sadie said. 'It won't be easy to play dumb when Aitkens is across the table from you.'

'Consider it done,' I said smugly.

'I wouldn't be so cocky,' Sadie warned. 'Keeping a blank face while people fire questions at you is not easy.'

'You've never sat next to me in maths class.'

'His dumb act is very convincing,' Hussein sighed. 'Natural, you might say.'

'See? Told ya,' I crowed.

Keeping our powers a secret was even more important now. The less our parents knew, the better. We couldn't risk anyone finding out about us. It would only put everyone we loved in danger.

That meant no more half-days at Caversham.

There'd be no more thumping wins for Lady P's this week and I could kiss my flying lessons goodbye too – for now, anyway. The building was being watched and so were we. We were on official superpower lockdown. Huddled together on the roof terrace, it was hard not to feel uneasy. We had got so used to thinking we were safe up here, invisible to the rest of the world.

Maybe we weren't.

We said goodbye to each other and left the roof in silence.

When I got back downstairs, the flat was empty. Mum had left for work and Granny was out.

I went straight to the sitting room and pulled my suitcase out from under the sofa.

Opening it, I burrowed under folded shirts and

stacks of pants until I came to a single red and white football sock. I removed the jar of sweets stuffed into its heel.

Unscrewing its lid, I plucked out one sweet and rolled it between my fingers. Her whiskers twitching, Lemon stirred and sauntered over.

If I pressed its jellied sides together, I could feel the capsule inside, a tiny round ball that shouldn't be there. Inside that thin sheath was a drop of the most precious juice in the world. One sip and – *presto chango* – the hidden powers inside someone would be unleashed.

How much would a person pay to possess a superpower?

A million pounds?

A hundred million?

A billion?

More?

I licked the frosting off my finger and put the sweet back into the jar. Stuffing the jar in turn back inside my football sock, I tied a maroon KEEP CALM AND AVOID ZOMBIES T-shirt around it. Then I buried the T-shirt under more clothes and closed the suitcase.

No one would ever think of looking here. Would they?

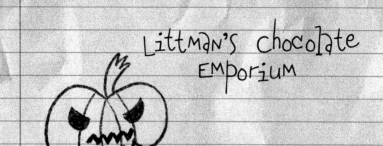

Littman's Chocolate Emporium

The next day, Hussein and I legged it over to Littman's Chocolate Emporium – London's most famous sweet shop – after school.

We got as far as their front door.

Behind a high glass window that stretched to the corner, there hung a crinkly orange and black sign. It said: **HALLOWEEN IS COMING.** *Witches and ghouls should never go hungry*. Underneath it, Jack-o'-lanterns glowed, silhouettes of witches flew on broomsticks and paper skeletons danced over a London skyline made entirely of chocolate.

Hussein and I pressed our noses against the glass.

'Where would you start?' he asked me.

'Big Ben.' It had a marzipan clock-face and hands made from the darkest chocolate. The tower was a chocolate praline core covered in golden flakes. 'I'd start there, then work my way through the Houses of Parliament. You?'

Hussein wet his lips. 'The London Eye,' he said, pointing to the huge Ferris wheel on the other side of the Thames, which was a swirling chocolate river. 'They say each passenger capsule has a different flavour – chilli-chocolate, lemongrass and ginger, chocolate nougat – thirty-two of them in all. Plus the spindle is made of vanilla truffle.'

'Good choice.'

Mouths watering, we wrenched ourselves away from the window and entered the shop.

People travelled from all over England to dunk a mug into a tall seven-tier chocolate fountain that oozed rich, creamy milk chocolate, or roam aisles of candy canes and marshmallows and lollipops, filling their trollies with goodies. And the smell! There were heaps of cinnamon swirls, butterscotch toffee dripping with caramel, countertops piled high with chunks of triple-chocolate brownies, and marzipan slices sprinkled with shavings of almonds and oranges. The moment you entered, a whiff alone was a sugar rush.

In the 'New World' aisle, we found mango

fizz-balls and Brazilian peanut brittle, pineapple cakes and coconut candies. The Nature's Own section was on the middle shelf. There wasn't much to choose from: a few bags of chocolate peanuts, peppermint gumballs, banana almond fudge in a green, recyclable box – and one dusty jar of jellied mints with a Peruvian warrior on them.

We grabbed the jar.

I picked up four Snap Fizzles on my way to the till – one each for Sadie, Hussein, me and Mum. When we stepped outside, Hussein and I tore into ours, tossing the gumballs into our mouths.

Pop! Fizzle! Snap!

Standing in front of Littman's, we wallowed in our gumballs' savoury delights, chewing away like two goats in a field. It was a top-notch dining moment, but soon disturbed by a voice I knew all too well.

'Well,' Mulch smirked. 'Isn't this a pleasant surprise?'

Hardly.

Even worse, Mulch was not alone. His gang of braying half-wits were there too.

'I didn't expect to see you here,' Mulch sneered

as his minions made a circle around us. 'What did you get?'

'Snap Fizzles,' I said. 'Like a firecracker going off in your mouth.'

'Let me try one,' he said quickly.

'Sorry, Mulch. I can't do that. I only have two left and I'm saving those for— Hey!'

Someone behind me snatched the bag of Snap Fizzles out of my hand and threw them to Mulch.

'You like these, do you?' Grinning, Mulch stuffed both gumballs into his mouth at once. His cheeks bulged. He made a great show of it too, his eyes wide, struggling to chew because his mouth was so full.

And then he spat them out on to the footpath. 'Sorry, Sweeney,' he said. 'They're not for me.'

His mates sniggered.

Sparks began to ping from my fingertips.

'Look at how red his face is!' Mulch laughed.

Steam hissed from my armpits.

'Are you blushing, Sweeney? Not going to cry are you?'

I swallowed a mouthful of flames and fixed him with a fiery glare. 'Mulch,' I said, 'prepare to meet your Maker.'

big brother

Before I could smite Mulch down with a blast of fire, Hussein jumped between us.

'You can't do this,' he pleaded with me. Placing his hands on my chest, he tried to hold me back.

It wasn't easy.

'Ow! Ow! Ow!' he cried, his hands fluttering away whenever he touched me. 'Ow!'

'What's wrong, Aziz? Sweeney may be ugly, but his face isn't *that* painful.'

The minions hooted and hollered. Mulch lapped it up. He swaggered forward, pointing at me and making rude gestures.

'Forget him,' Hussein said to me. 'Show him you're the bigger man and walk away. We don't need to stay here. We've got the sweets we came for.'

Mulch's ratty ears twitched at this. Spotting the jar tucked into my blazer pocket, his tiny eyes narrowed. 'What do you have there?' he asked.

I placed a hand over my pocket. 'Forget it, Mulch. There is NO WAY you are touching this.'

Mulch backed off, stunned by my defiant tone.

The same, however, could not be said of the pea-brains who followed him around.

'Ooooooh,' they chorused.

One of his crew said, 'Come on, Mulch! You can't let him get away with that!'

'Show him who's boss, Mulch!' another shouted.

'Fight! Fight! Fight!' they chanted.

Buoyed by their cheers, Mulch played to the crowd. 'Sweeney, it looks like I'm going to have to teach you a lesson,' he crowed. As he rolled up his sleeves, I weighed the pros and cons of blasting him to kingdom come.

PRO	CON
It would feel WONDERFUL!	The police, I expect, would not look kindly on me turning a fellow citizen into a small pile of ash.

Revenge is SWEET!	Mum would be disappointed in me. So would Sadie and Hussein.
Mulch would NEVER bother me again!	I would not enjoy prison.

Fire or no fire? Endure Mulch or put an end to him?

It was in the balance.

Even Steven.

Too close to call.

And then Hussein surprised me.

Leaning towards me, he whispered, 'Don't worry, mate. I've got this. You get that jar home. I'll take care of Mulch.'

I blinked, taken aback by his offer.

Are there greater examples of bravery in history? I don't think so. Step aside, Richard the Lion-Heart. Back of the line, Frodo Baggins. Make way for Hussein Aziz.

Hussein knew – as I did – that he couldn't fight his way out of a paper bag and yet, here he was, offering to take my place. *That's* what I call bravery.

Fortunately, another hero happened by.

A great shadow fell over us, a shadow so vast it blotted out the sun and threw half the street into darkness.

'FOOL! It is you!' he thundered, striding towards me, his mighty muscles flexed. 'It is I, ATLAS!'

Mouths opened.

Jaws dropped.

We gaped up in wonder at the man-mountain who had entered our midst.

'Hey, Atlas,' I said. 'How goes it?'

'It goes well, Fool. I am off to the market to purchase oil for my skin.' He ran a hand over the boulder that was his bicep. 'Strong men must moisturise.'

As I thanked Atlas for the tip, a deliciously cunning plan suddenly made itself known to me, one that would put Mulch in his rightful place – under my heel. All I needed to do was play the fool, a cowardly one. Launching myself at Atlas, I clung to the rock face he called a waistline like a frightened rabbit.

'Fool!' he cried. 'What is wrong? You are trembling!'

'Atlas,' I said, my voice shaking, 'you and I are friends, right?'

'We are more than friends, Fool,' Atlas said, thumping the wide plains of his chest. 'We are circus brothers now.'

'Good. I'm glad to hear that, brother Atlas, because I could use your help.' Fixing Mulch in my cross-hairs, I raised a finger and pointed it at him. 'THAT KID IS TRYING TO STEAL MY MINTS!'

Reader, the look of wide-eyed, white-faced, pants-wetting terror which splashed across Mulch's face at that very moment is one I will treasure for years to come. Even now, as I jot this tale into my spiral notebook, I must set my pen aside and chuckle long and hard.

Grabbing Mulch by the neck, Atlas hoisted the little git into the air. 'You are bad boy,' Atlas said, shaking him about.

I stopped trembling, my spirits mightily revived, and glanced around at the others. Hussein, as you might expect, was in wonderful form, hooting and hollering. But what of those boys and girls who Mulch called friends?

Did they beg Atlas to let him go?

Did they gang together and threaten to rush at the strongman Hussein-style, risking life and limb to save their mate?

No. They got out their phones and took photos. All of them.

Tips on how to get along with others #2:
Loyal friends stand up for you when you need them most.

They posed beside Atlas. They took selfies with Mulch jiggling behind them. Pleased to see so many cameras pointed at him, Atlas hammed it up too. He pulled faces. He posed and flexed. He dangled Mulch in front of them like a carrot on a stick.

We were soon joined by Joe Jackson. Rounding the corner with a smoothie in one hand, Jackson took one look at Mulch in mid-air and nearly swallowed his straw. Never one to be caught out on a losing side, Jackson joined me and Hussein on the footpath. In fact, it was Jackson who suggested some form of punishment was in order once he heard Mulch was caught trying to nick my sweets.

'How else will Mitchell learn the error of his ways?' he said.

A street-style Olympic event was proposed, one which involved Atlas throwing Mulch as far as he could. All of us were up for this, including the turncoats Mulch called friends.

'Tell Atlas to aim for the canal,' Jackson said. 'With a good run-up, he ought to clear the wall from here.'

'Jackson,' I said, 'you are on fire today. Who else is in?'

There were roars of approval. Atlas seemed up for it too, stretching his arm and practising his run-up. Two of Mulch's mates ran down to the canal to be ready to fish him out while the others jostled for best camera position. And then Mulch went and spoiled it all by blubbering about being not being able to swim and being too young to die, etcetera, etcetera. In the end, Atlas made him promise to be good and released him.

As soon as his feet hit the ground, Mulch sped off, and never once looked back.

Now that's what I call a happy ending.

routines and rehearsals

The next few days were manic. Everyone wanted a moment of my time.

Miss Spatchcock

Miss Spatchcock met me at the school gates and ushered me into her classroom each morning for 'Aidan Time'. Unhappy with my one-word replies to questions and accusing me (correctly) of abandoning my diary, Miss Spatchcock urged me to sign up for Creative Writing, a lunch-time club.

'Creative writing fosters critical thinking. It develops reading skills. It explores prose, poetry and scripts. And most of all,' Miss Spatchcock beamed, 'it's fun!'

I was not convinced. I preferred my lunch-times outdoors. Not only were they active, they were educational. Evading the marauding hordes of 4th and 5th Formers who skulked about in the Yard was an essential life skill for our part of North London.

Miss Spatchcock arched an eyebrow. 'Did I mention there's cake?'

'Cake?'

'Lots of it.' Miss Spatchcock tapped her iPad. Up popped a photo of biscuits, fudge and brownies on a tray. 'Chocolate fuels the mind.'

Memories of Littman's came flooding back. 'Well,' I said. 'I might drop by.'

'Please do.'

So I did, that very afternoon, in fact. Seven girls were in Miss Spatchcock's classroom when I arrived. Each of them, I noted, was on the tall side.

Maybe there was something to this writing.

No one looked up when I entered, which was fine with me. I found a seat at the back near the cake spread. Between the lemon drizzle cake (a definite thumbs up) and arriving late, I didn't get far into my story before it was time to share with the room. That didn't stop Miss Spatchcock from applauding the one line I managed to write.

' "It began with a doorbell". I like it, Aidan, so full of mystery.'

The others had far more to say, mostly on how hard it was to be a young woman in Britain today. Unsurprisingly, I had little to add to this discussion, so I kept my head down instead, nodding sympathetically in the right places and moving on to the walnut cake (delicious) when no one was looking. I couldn't complain. Not only did I get a new spiral notebook, but Creative Writing gave me an excuse to avoid Mulch.

Mitchell Mulch

Brother Atlas had made quite an impression on Mulch. He spent the next day with his head down and his mouth shut. What bliss! What peace! School was almost bearable with a sulking Mulch.

It didn't last. When Mulch heard that Atlas worked at the circus, the questions started. How long was the circus in town? How did I meet Atlas and the other circus stars? Was the ringmaster a lion-tamer? Were the clowns funny? And one question which set alarm bells ringing – could I show him around?

Me?

Show Mulch around the circus?

Not a chance. He kept at it though. Nag, nag,

nag. The boy was planning something.

So was Granny.

Granny

Granny trusted no one. In her mind, the phone call Mum had received from Ash Aitkens was a plot to smuggle cash, drugs, bombs or god knows what else into the United Kingdom. It was her patriotic duty therefore to confiscate this parcel and examine its contents. Her choice of tools for this search – a saw, a hammer and a blow-torch – lacked a certain subtlety, but when it came to defending Britain's borders, Granny did not mess about. Stationing herself in the lobby, she took up sentry duty and waited for the parcel to be delivered.

It didn't come.

Days passed and still nothing arrived. No post. Not just for our flat either, but the whole apartment block. There were no letters or newspapers, no bills or leaflets. Nothing. Visitors stopped coming. Even residents stayed away.

How unusual, you say.

Might this have anything to do with the mad old

woman pacing the lobby floor with a saw, a hammer and a blow-torch in her hands?

Yes, reader. It might.

There was one silver lining though. Granny's one-woman barricade of the lobby meant she was less concerned with me. Without the She-Bear looking over my shoulder, I could spend as much time at the circus as I liked.

Zarathustra's Travelling Circus

Rehearsals in the Big Top were non-stop in the days leading up to Opening Night.

The Red Arrows, the family of seven Chinese gymnasts – the youngest seven years old, the oldest sixty-four – tumbled and spun on mats.

Gareth the magician, a wide-faced Welshman, practiced with his assistant, a black and white Border collie called Gladys. He tapped his wand and whistled, making her jump up and leap into his magic box in one bound. How he sawed Gladys in half – her head howling out of one box, her tail wagging out of the other – and then put her back together again, I'll never know.

Above us, Eshe and Rodrigo twisted and twirled

in the air. Dead-Eye stalked targets, her six-guns blazing, firing bull's-eyes at mad contraptions that whizzed and beeped. Kenise Williams prowled along a tight rope and brother Atlas grunted, shifting enormous dumb-bells over his head with each arm.

There were clowns too.

The Krazy Klowns

Donal, Shane and Finbar Kerrigan were the Krazy Klowns. The Kerrigans grew up on a small farm in County Kerry, Ireland, where they spent most of their childhood chasing each other up and down the fields – and occasionally through the house – with rakes, hoes, spades, tractors and any blunt instrument they could lay their hands on. When they finished school, the Kerrigan brothers travelled to London, hoping to find fame and fortune as stunt men.

For a time, they succeeded. Donal drove a motorcycle off a cliff in the film *Death Slide*. Shane jumped out of a helicopter in *Break Out IV*. Finbar staggered out of a flaming castle in the Netflix series, *Planet Apocalypse*.

Despite their success, the Kerrigan brothers discovered life as stunt men wasn't for them. They found no joy in being mauled, pummelled or stabbed by strangers. What they really missed, it seemed, was battering each other.

So they became the Krazy Klowns. Now they could bash, slap, pound and thump each other to their hearts' delight – just as they had so many years ago in Kerry – *and* get paid for it!

The Kerrigan brothers loved the circus.

So did Dmitri.

Dmitri

Each afternoon, Dmitri showed me the ropes – the rope for the prop box; the ropes for the high wire acts; the ropes that the magician used when his assistant vanished and reappeared; the lasso Dead-Eye spun in her Wild West act; the foot-ropes that steered the Krazy Kar so the Klowns could wave at the crowd as they drove; and the ropes that operated the maze of secret entrances and exits inside the Big Top.

The circus stars often stopped to chat. I was 'Fool' to them, not Aidan, skipping after Dmitri like a court jester in a history book on life in a medieval castle.

Not that I minded. I learned loads being around

Dmitri – and not just about ropes either. About how spotlights worked and how carousels turned and when to be firm with instructions and when to take the advice of others. Dmitri was more than just a ringmaster. He was good and kind and fair. I'd play his Fool any day.

If only I didn't have the arrival of Ash Aitkens and the fake parcel hanging over me.

Sadie

Putting the fake parcel together called for careful planning, attention to detail and precision wrapping, which is why I asked Sadie to do it.

She came round after school one day and laid out what she needed – bubble wrap, tape, brown paper, the stamps. She began by draping the new jar of Nature's Own in bubble wrap, then looping Sellotape around it. We squeezed this lump into the original box (I had kept it hidden under the sofa) and curled the information booklet around it. After sliding the box into an envelope, Sadie wrote the words 'Ultra-secreto' on it in red marker. The brown wrapping paper came next. After carefully cutting out the Peruvian stamps I had

saved (I liked the llamas. They looked so cuddly.),
she glued them on to the corner of the parcel.
Next, Sadie copied out my name and address in
purple ink and in the same loopy handwriting.
Last of all, she wrinkled the brown paper, so it
looked worn and travelled.

Sadie held the fake parcel up to me. 'What do
you think?'

I turned it over. 'There's a career for you in
forgery, should you ever choose a life of crime.'

'Thanks.'

'I mean it, Sadie. Aitkens will never spot the
difference.'

It fooled Mum too.

Mum

Mum was sitting up in bed that night, her legs
curled under her. There was a cup of tea on her
bedside table and a book open in her hands.

I gave her the parcel that Sadie had wrapped.

'So this is it! The mysterious present,' she said.
'You did well to get it past your grandmother.'

'Sadie helped.'

I watched her hold the parcel up to the light and

examine it. She turned it over.

'Are you looking forward to opening this?' Mum asked me.

I shuffled my feet. 'Yes.'

'So am I.' Mum wrapped her arms around the parcel like it was a brown teddy bear. She closed her eyes.

I turned to go.

'Your father loved you very much, Aidan. You know that, don't you?'

'Yes.'

'Promise me that you'll never forget him.'

'I won't.'

When I closed her door, she was where I had left her, still cradling the parcel, her eyes closed.

Hussein

Unlike Sadie or me, Hussein could use his computo-power whenever he wanted and no one would be the wiser. Stick a laptop screen in front of him or put a phone in his hand and he looked like any other twelve year old.

So ... did Hussein use this time to further computer technology or advance the formatting of electrical circuits in new and exciting ways?

No.

He logged on to *Jedi Academy VI* and gamed non-stop, achieving his lifelong dream – Jedi Master status – in record time. When he put down his phone at last, there were tears in his eyes.

In fairness, Hussein also kept close watch on Ash Aitkens. He monitored his texts, he read his emails and he listened to his conversations on the phone. That meant we not only knew when his plane landed, but which cab he took from the airport.

And it meant that when Aitkens rang our doorbell, Sadie, Hussein and I were waiting for him.

a citizen's arrest

'Hello! Anyone home?'

I took a deep breath.

On the sofa, Sadie crossed her legs, coolly guarding my suitcase, her school satchel and its stash of weapons on the floor beside her. Opposite Sadie, Hussein sat trembling in the armchair.

We were ready.

I pressed the entrance buzzer. 'Come in. We're on the 3rd floor, flat D.'

Down the hall, a bedroom door opened. Out came Mum in a blue skirt, her cheeks shining and black eyeliner on. She was even wearing lipstick!

'What do you think?' Mum did a small twirl which Sadie answered by waving her arms and rocking her hips. 'Turquoise is so your colour,' she trilled. 'You look gorgeous, Mrs Sweeney!'

'Very smart,' Hussein agreed.

I made a gesture usually associated with puking.

Ugh. Dressing up for Ash Aitkens? Lipstick? What was she thinking? I had half a mind to smoke that loser the moment he walked through the door.

Mum stopped in front of me. 'What's wrong with you?'

'Nothing,' I lied.

'It doesn't look like it.'

I said nothing.

'If your face got any longer, it would be on the floor. I would have thought you'd be excited to see what your father left you.'

'I am.'

Mum's bottom lip curled down as her right eyebrow arrowed up. It was a look I knew well.

A translation of Mum's expression:

It was official notification that my behaviour had been deemed 'suspicious'. I was now under surveillance which meant any words or gestures I used could be held as evidence against me. Interrogations loomed.

Knuckles rapped against the outside of our front door.

'Hello?' came a voice from the hallway. 'Ash Aitkens here. Anyone home?'

Mum inspected her image in the mirror one last time and let him in.

Aitkens was tanned from the sun and taller than I'd expected. He had a tailored suit on under a black cashmere overcoat. Flashing Mum a pearly-white smile, he stepped into our hallway.

Mum showed him into the sitting room.

'You must be Aidan,' he grinned. 'You're the image of your dad.' He gripped my hand hard and shook it. 'He spoke about you a lot, young man.'

I let go of his hand. 'That's funny. I don't ever remember him mentioning you.'

Still smiling, Aitkens winked at Mum. 'I'm glad to hear that.'

'What Aidan means,' Mum said quickly, 'is that Seamus rarely talked about the Army when he was home. He always said they were two worlds that should never collide.'

'That sounds like Seamus. A man of principle, he was, and no one knows that better than me.' Aitkens ruffled my hair. 'He was an outstanding soldier and an example to the men who served beside him.'

Mum beamed.

Aitkens jutted his thumb at Sadie and Hussein. 'Who are these two fine young people, friends of yours?'

'Yes!' Sadie said, flashing him a smile. 'I'm Sadie. I live upstairs and I can't wait to see what's inside that parcel! Aidan hasn't stopped talking about it since it arrived.'

Hussein was more guarded. 'Hello,' he squeaked, wiping a bead of sweat from his forehead. 'Welcome to London.'

Aitkens rubbed his hands together. 'It's good to be back. Seeing that we all know each other now, let's have a look at that package.'

'Follow me,' Mum said, walking into the kitchen. 'I left it in here. I had to hide it in case my mother-in-law . . .' Mum stopped. Her eyes darted from side to side. 'Have any of you seen Granny?'

As if on cue, the closet door burst open and out jumped Granny, stick high and vengeance in her heart. How long the old girl was waiting there in the dark, I can't say, but she wasted no time making herself known.

Thump! Crack! Wallop!

Granny gave Ash Aitkens three swift ones – one to the head, one to the shoulders and one to the back of the knees – with her walking stick, and down he went.

As introductions go, it was short and brutal, but then Granny never was one for ceremony. No polite chit-chat or handshakes for her! It was more like, 'Ash Aitkens, say hello to my stick.' In fact, as I watched her standing over him – snorting like a mad grizzly, her stick raised – I experienced a rare moment of warmth for Granny. Yes, the She-Bear made my life a misery, but like any powerful and volatile weapon, I realised that, pointed in the right direction (i.e. away from me and at someone else), she could be useful.

Sadie and Hussein rushed over for a peek. From the three of us, it was big smiles all around.

Mum, however, was not pleased.

'Have you lost hold of your senses?' she shouted, stepping over the semi-conscious Ash Aitkens and facing Granny. 'What do you think you're doing?'

Granny poked Ash's ribs with her foot. 'This is a citizen's arrest. I am apprehending a burglar.'

'A burglar? Are you mad?' Mum cried. 'He rang the doorbell. He knocked at the door! I let him in!'

'He's a thief,' Granny growled. 'I trust my nose. He reeks of crime and mischief.'

His cologne smelt of oak and vanilla to me, but who was I to argue?

Aitkens groaned and rolled over. He rubbed his head.

'Granny! Granny!' I shouted. 'He's waking up!'

In other words, *Quick! Here's your chance. Finish him off!*

Blood up, helmet-hair on end, Granny gripped her stick. A battle-frenzy was on her and I, for one, was not getting in her way. I backed away to give the She-Bear space to launch an attack.

Mum was made of sterner stuff though.

'Put that down, old woman, or I swear it's the Home for you.'

Granny's twitchy eye slowed. Grumbling, her single eyebrow drooped and she lowered her stick.

Even the She-Bear knew better than to mess with Mum.

The Gut-cruncher

Mum gave Ash Aitkens an ice pack, which he held to the lump poking out of his forehead.

'I should report that madwoman to the police,' he snarled. 'I have half a mind to sue.'

We were in the kitchen. Mum and Granny were on one side of the table, Sadie and Hussein the other. I was at one end with Lemon in my lap and Aitkens was next to me. One lump over the head – well, three actually – and the brute had begun showing us his true colours. He hadn't stopped complaining since we dragged him off the floor and propped him up in the chair. I, for one, had heard my fill.

'Come on,' I said. 'It wasn't that bad. It wasn't as if Granny hit you with a crowbar.'

'You weren't unconscious *that* long,' Sadie said, joining in. 'Five, ten seconds, tops.'

Hussein agreed. 'Blink and you missed it.'

Mum shot us a glance. It seemed she wanted us to leave the small talk to her. 'There's no need for that, Ash. My mother-in-law made a mistake, that's all. Isn't that right, Hilda?'

Granny picked up the bread knife and waved it. 'I'm old and confused,' she crowed. 'Who knows what I might do next?'

'Ha, ha, ha. No more of your little jokes,' Mum said, taking the knife from Granny's hand. 'Ash might think you're serious.'

'I am capable of a surprise or two myself,' Aitkens said, cracking his knuckles and fixing Granny with an evil glare.

'And who doesn't love a surprise?' Mum said cheerfully. 'I know I do!'

Aitkens removed the ice pack from his forehead. As he placed it on the table, I noticed some blue and green markings on his wrist.

Granny saw it too. 'Is that a scar under your palm?' she asked him.

'This?' He unbuttoned his cuff and rolled up his sleeve. 'It's my monkey.'

Inked into his wrist in blue and green was a

long-tailed monkey. When Aitkens flexed his hand, it looked as if the monkey's mouth opened, revealing a set of fangs.

'I'm afraid the story of how I got this,' Aitkens said with a smirk to Mum, 'is one for adults' ears only.'

'My stepsister has tats,' Sadie said, leaning forward to examine it. 'What made you decide on a monkey?'

Aitkens combed his hair back with his fingers. 'Monkeys are much like me: cheeky, quick, far more intelligent than they first appear and fond of grooming.'

Hussein said, 'Not all monkeys are playful.'

'Very true,' Aitkens said. 'Cape baboons, for example, are well-known for their ferocity. Only the strongest survive in their troops.' His eyes narrowing, he smiled wistfully at Granny. 'What a shame we humans choose to live by different rules.'

Granny gripped the head of her walking stick so tight her knuckles went white. 'If it's a fight you want, you've come to the right person,' she snarled.

Aitkens bristled and the grin slipped from his

face. 'You *dare* to challenge me?'

It looked like we were heading for Round Two, which was fine by me.

Then Mum went and spoiled it all.

'Anyone for tea?' she asked.

There was a long, tense silence as Granny and the challenger faced off across the kitchen table.

Aitkens blinked first.

'Three sugars,' he said. 'Milky and sweet, that's how I like it.'

If ever there was a time for the old girl to reach for the gin, this was it. The moment had passed though. She eased off.

'I'll have a cuppa,' Granny grunted at Mum.

Aitkens rubbed his shoulder. 'Is there any chance of a bite to eat as well? A sandwich will do. I'm not long off my plane.'

I passed Lemon to Sadie.

'Don't worry, Mum. I'll get this.'

I had a sandwich in mind.

'The Gut-Cruncher', from *The Poisoner's Cookbook*:

Here's a deadly takeaway no one orders twice.

A few bites from this lethal concoction and you can kiss that that pesky blighter goodbye!

1) Take two slices of mouldy bread. Smother with rancid butter
2) Fill a cup with earthworms, cockroaches and woodlice. Crush in a bowl. Add a teaspoon of powdered mouse and, if available, a toad's innards
3) Pour in a teaspoon of loo cleaner and stir continuously for three minutes. When the mixture is good and runny, spread over bread.
4) Top with a leaf of raw cabbage
5) Season with Tabasco sauce and garnish with shavings of cat poop

Best served in a badly-lit room.

'Leave it, son,' Aitkens said, grabbing me by the arm. 'Your mother will see to it.' He pointed at the hissing Lemon (who had taken an instant dislike to him). 'I'm not fond of cat hairs in my food.'

Mum said, 'Aidan, since you're up, why don't you get Ash the parcel?'

I snuck a glance at Sadie, who winked back. Hussein closed his eyes and hid his head. Breezing

223

over to the cupboard, I found the fake parcel where I'd left it, on the bottom shelf. I handed it to Aitkens.

He stood. Turning his back on us, Aitkens held it up to the light. He inspected the stamps. He studied the postmarks. He examined its handwriting. When he turned around, he wore a manic grin. 'You would not believe what I went through to get my hands on this.'

'That's a story I'd *love* to hear,' Sadie said.

'Me too,' Hussein and I said together.

'I'd rather be roasted over a fire than listen to this idiot natter on,' Granny snorted.

'That can be arranged, old woman,' Aitkens replied.

Mum plopped the teapot down between them and handed Aitkens a plate with a cheese sandwich on it. 'Now that we're all happy, shall we open the parcel?'

'Yes,' Aitkens grinned. 'Let's.'

Swap

I pulled the parcel closer.

Everyone leaned in. Mum got out of her chair and stood next to me. I could practically hear her heart thumping with excitement.

I was nervous too. My fingers were so hot that I scorched the brown-papered wrapping when I touched it. Afraid I'd burn the parcel before I could open it, I grabbed the bread knife and cut into it. The wad of bubble wrap popped out. I sliced through that and the Sellotape too, ripping it open to reveal . . . a small wooden box.

Aitkens chuckled. 'Kid, you should see your face. What were you expecting, football boots?'

No. I was expecting sweets. I stared dumbly at the box, unsure what to do. Luckily, Mum was there. She reached across me and opened it. Out popped a toy drummer in a red Horse Guard's uniform. As soon as the lid was extended, a scratchy 'God Save the Queen' began to play. His little drumsticks started tapping.

'It's a music box!' Mum cried.

I stared at the toy drummer in disbelief. It was a fake fake parcel!

Ears up, Lemon hopped on to the table, her tail swishing from side to side. Mum, Hussein, Sadie and I huddled nearer. Even Granny leaned forward for a peek.

'Look! There's an inscription,' Mum said, pointing at a thin metal label attached to the rim of the frame where the words *Property of Seamus A. Sweeney* were carved.

Mum was beside herself. 'Oh, Seamus,' she said, half-giggling, half-sobbing as the toy drummer banged his drum. 'You mad, silly man.' Rushing across the room, Mum threw her arms around Ash Aitkens. 'Thank you. Thank you,' she cried. 'You don't know how much . . .'

She didn't finish.

I fell back into my chair. I had anticipated many different outcomes for my face-off with Ash Aitkens – some splendid, others awful. It is safe to say that seeing him with his arm wrapped around Mum's waist and winking at me as he said, 'Think of your old Uncle Ash when you open that box,' was not one of them.

Dabbing her eye with a tissue, Mum broke free of Aitkens' grasp. 'How well did you know Seamus?'

Aitkens popped a corner of his sandwich into his mouth and chewed. 'We were never very close. I spent most of my time in the officers' barracks, so I didn't see much of Corporal Sweeney. I was never one for mixing with the enlisted men, you know. Bad for morale. Everyone should keep to their own, I say.'

'Lance Corporal,' Mum corrected. 'Seamus was a Lance Corporal.'

Aitkens ignored her and prattled on. 'Fortune tied us together, however. I can honestly say that if it weren't for Seamus Sweeney, I would not be here today.'

'Fortune?' I asked.

'Destiny,' Mum explained. 'The belief some people have that our fates are written in the stars.' She turned to Aitkens. 'So what is it that tied you and Seamus together?'

'His accident. You see, your husband was never

supposed to be in that jeep the day he died. I was.'

The kitchen fell silent. All I could hear was the ticking of the clock and Ash Aitkens chewing his way through the rest of his sandwich. Mum stared out the window. Granny sagged forward, clutching her walking stick. Sadie reached for my hand under the table, her long brown fingers knitting together with my stubby pink hand. Hussein sat dazed in his chair and Lemon hopped into my lap, nuzzling her head against my arm.

Only Aitkens seemed unbothered. It was as if, now that the parcel was opened, the mask he used to charm people with had been set aside. The real Ash Aitkens – the vain, money-grubbing, deceitful side of him which Sadie and Hussein had shown me – was out in the open for all to see.

Aitkens carried on with his story. 'I had overslept, you see. I had a late night with the lads – a game of golf that got out of hand. Ha, ha. I could barely get out of bed the next morning, so I asked for a volunteer to take my place. Step forward, Corporal Sweeney.'

'Lance Corporal,' Mum said through gritted teeth. '*Lance* Corporal Sweeney.'

He rattled on about how sorry he was and what a terrible loss it had been, how Dad had died for his country. Blah, blah, blah. I stopped listening after a while. I had heard this stuff countless times before.

'Tell us about the music box,' Mum said, her gaze still fixed on the window.

'The least I could do was clear out your husband's locker,' Aitkens said. 'That's when I came across the music box. What can I say? It's a fine piece of craftsmanship and I took a fancy to it.' Aitkens picked the box off the table and twirled it around. 'Plus it reminded me of my dance with death. This box inspired me, it drove me on. It convinced me I was put on this earth for a reason.'

'So why have you returned it now after all this time?' Mum said angrily. 'Was your conscience getting the better of you?'

'Hardly,' Aitkens sniggered. 'An opportunity arose, you might say. I help you, you help me.' His chest swelled. He pushed his sandwich plate aside and straightened his back. 'I have stumbled on to a rare fortune. I am ready to seize my destiny. Soon the whole world will know the great powers I possess.'

At the mention of 'powers', my arms and chest

tingled. Glancing at Sadie and Hussein, I could see they felt the same.

Granny, however, was not in a tingling mood. She slapped the table and hooted. 'Pull the other one!' she cackled. 'Destiny? Powers? The boy's cat has more sense than a loser like you!'

'What would you know about great men and their destinies, you old bat?' Aitkens tugged on the lapels of his overcoat and straightened his tie. 'I am finally bounding forward with my life. I no longer need keepsakes and souvenirs to spur me on.'

Granny poked the pocket of his overcoat with her stick. 'Souvenirs like this, you mean?'

His smug grin vanished. Clutching the pocket of his coat, Aitkens scrambled away so quickly he upended the chair.

'I told you he was a cheat! The *real* parcel – the one that was delivered to this flat – is hidden in his coat.' Granny stood and waved her stick menacingly, slicing it through the air like a sword.

'Get away from me!' Aitkens shrieked. 'I don't know what you're talking about!'

'Yes, you do. You're nothing but a nasty little pickpocket!'

Stick raised, Granny charged.

Aitkens raced for the door. As he ran past us, he snatched the bread knife off the table.

'Pocket this, old woman!' he cried and, without breaking stride, he hurled the knife at Granny.

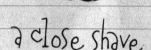

a close shave

The knife hit Granny above her eyes and stuck there.

I screamed.

Mum shrieked.

Hussein collapsed backwards into his chair.

Granny stared up at the knife sticking out of her forehead.

Finally, Mum – our health care professional – examined the offending area. She found, much to her surprise, that there was no wound, not even a mark. As soon as Mum touched the bread knife, it gave way, dropping into her hand. If it weren't for the part now dividing Granny's long, hairy eyebrow into two, you would never believe it had happened.

Did Granny's hairy eyebrow stop the bread knife?

No, of course not. It was Sadie. She stopped the knife with her power.

'I didn't mean to scare you,' she told us afterwards. 'I was focusing so hard on stopping the bread knife that it got stuck. I couldn't move it.'

I was more worried about Mum than Granny. Black smears streaked both cheeks. Though she seemed pale, her cheeks were patchy and red.

'I'm sorry for exposing you to that horrid man,' Mum said, apologising to Sadie and Hussein. 'Thank goodness everyone is safe.'

'Should we call the police?' I asked.

'No,' Granny snarled. 'Leave him to me.' She thundered past, stick in hand. 'Don't wait up,' she said ominously. 'I may be late.'

Sadie, Hussein and I cheered her on as she barrelled out the door. Granny finding Ash Aitkens would solve all our problems. I, of course, had more important matters to contend with. It was, after all . . . OPENING NIGHT AT THE CIRCUS!

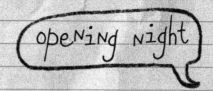
opening night

Spotlights swivelled overhead. Carnival music blared. The neon FORTUNE-TELLER sign on Mathilde's caravan lit up the sky and the twinkly white lights that hung around the circus tent lit up the Heath.

I came across a woman in black on my way to the Wild West shooting gallery. Black dress, black hair, black make-up, black nails, black eyes. A blood-red pendant hung from her neck and gaudy rings crowded her fingers.

''Ello,' she said. 'Are you ready for zis evening's show?'

'*Mathilde?*'

'Yes.'

'You look different.'

She arched a haughty eyebrow. 'Zis is my costume. Fortune-tellers must dress up too. You like?'

Fortune-teller? Stick a hat with evil horns on her head and she could have passed for Maleficent. If she had shown up in that outfit when we first met, I would have high-tailed it out the door and never looked back.

'You look ace,' I said.

Mathilde shrugged. 'I am French. I am always "ace".'

From the pocket of her dress she withdrew a pack of cards. 'We 'ave a custom at Zarathustra's on opening night, one zat goes back many years. Zee fortune-teller gives free reading. Very short. One card only.' She flipped the deck of tarot cards over, shuffling them with one hand. Her cards were old and worn, their edges soft.

'Would zee Fool like to try?'

'Why not?' I said.

Mathilde shuffled again, spinning and sliding the cards from hand to hand so fast they became one large blur. Flicking her wrist, she spread the cards into a giant fan. 'Pick one.'

I did.

It was the Tower.

Mathilde said, 'With you, it is always fire.'

I eyed the smoking tower uneasily. 'This doesn't look good.'

'It isn't,' Mathilde said, shaking her head.

Behind the black make-up, her green eyes softened. 'Be careful, little Fool. Zis is a card of danger. Expect zee unexpected.'

With Mathilde's warnings ringing in my ears, I walked carefully to the shooting gallery where Dead-Eye was waiting for me, her cowboy hat drawn down over her eyes.

'Hello, partner. Y'all ready for the big showdown?'

'Yes, ma'am!'

In the Wild West shooting gallery, Dead-Eye showed boys and girls how to hold the air rifles and aim them at targets. I was tasked with shouting,

'Yeehaw!' whenever a target was hit, and fetching the prizes when needed. Dead-Eye collected the money.

Soon the circus was buzzing. The band marched by, tooting their horns and strumming their guitars. The dancers shimmied after them in their sparkly suits and dresses. Dmitri appeared in his black top hat and red tail-coat, welcoming people as they queued for rides on the carousel and offering balloons to small children as they walked through the gate.

The crowd swelled. More people clamoured for a go at the shooting gallery or stood behind the shooters, cheering them on. I was so busy handing out prizes and shouting 'Yeehaw!' that I didn't spot Mum until she was in front of me.

Sadie and Hussein were there too. Mum made us pose for photos: beside the stall, holding an air rifle, standing next to Dead-Eye, and one with the three of us hugging a giant stuffed bear. At one point, Dmitri walked past and posed for a photo with me. While he and Mum chatted alone, the three of us put our heads together. Three hours had passed since Ash Aitkens had raced out of our flat and I was keen to hear some news.

Hussein held out his phone. 'You want a laugh? Have a look at this.'

'Are these Aitkens' texts?' I asked.

'They are.'

Sadie and I crowded closer.

'Our friend is meeting a sheikh, an internet billionaire and a media tycoon at the Ritz tonight. A crate of champagne has been ordered. Apparently there's a celebration.' Hussein held out his phone. On screen was a text he had intercepted:

Friends! Come to the great unveiling tonight. You will not be disappointed. AA

The urge to throw my hands in the air and fire a cannon of flames into the sky was so great that I had to swallow a mouthful of hot smoke before I could speak.

'This is good,' I spluttered. 'This is very good.'

Sadie said, 'I would love to see his face when he discovers there are no capsules in those mints.'

'Same.'

Mum returned with a programme. 'That Dmitri is *such* a nice man. Look what he gave me.'

ZARATHUSTRA'S TRAVELLING CIRCUS

proudly presents:
A PROGRAMME OF ATTRACTIONS
for your entertainment and enjoyment:

.... ⁘ ....

The legendary ringmaster and animal trainer,
DMITRI and his cast of thousands!

See the opening Grand Parade
of Circus Performers

Applaud the amazing gymnast family,
THE RED ARROWS

Marvel at **ATLAS**,
the Strongest Man Alive

Gasp at **ESHE** and **RODRIGO**,
the World's Greatest Dance Trapeze Artists

Be astonished by **GARETH the MAGICIAN**
and his wonder dog, **GLADYS**

Cheer on **DEAD-EYE**,
the Best Shot in the West

Be thrilled by **KENISE 'THE CAT'
WILLIAMS**, Rope-Walker

Have your breath taken away
by the stupendous **FINALE**

Featuring the Kings of Slapstick Comedy,
THE KRAZY KLOWNS

Sing and dance with
**THE ZARATHSUTRA'S CIRCUS
BAND AND DANCERS!**

And don't forget – visit
THE MYSTERIOUS MATHILDE
to get your fortunes read.
Drop-in or by appointment!

**PLUS – FIREWORKS! CARNIVAL GAMES!
FUN FOR ALL THE FAMILY!**

Suddenly, a loudspeaker crackled on and the carnival music died down.

'Ladies and gentlemen, boys and girls, please take your seats. This evening's performance is about to begin.'

fireworks

Tiny sparks flicked off my forearms and steam rose from my neck. I felt like a volcano ready to burst!

Mum wished me luck and I waved goodbye to Sadie and Hussein.

It was time for the Grand Parade!

The circus stars assembled at the performers' entrance. Dmitri was at the front, a thumb stuck into the pocket of his waistcoat. Eshe and Rodrigo, in matching red sequins, were behind, and the Krazy Klowns were next, their faces painted white and wearing shabby suits and ties. Everyone else waited behind until Dmitri gave the signal. I stood at the rear in my own circus costume – a red jersey with a gold Z in the front. I was so excited it was all I could do to keep from exploding into flames.

Boom! Rat-a-tat! Boom!

Drums thumped, trumpets blared.

242

The curtains opened. The circus stars entered the Big Top and the crowd went wild.

Dmitri doffed his hat to the crowd as the cast made a circle around him. 'Welcome to our circus,' he cried. 'We have travelled around the world three times – yes, three times – and now Zarathustra's Travelling Circus returns to London and its great people. Prepare yourself for the greatest show on earth. Our circus will amaze you! It shall astound and delight! This will be a night to remember! And now, please meet the performers.'

He introduced each performer, who waved at the audience when the spotlight fell on them in turn. When Dmitri finished, the performers trotted off and the Big Top went dark except for a swirl of red and gold spotlights. Asian hip-hop boomed from the speakers and in zoomed Li Jun Yang and his family of gymnasts. The Red Arrows had arrived.

The rest of the evening whizzed by.

Though I was busy – there were props to cart in and out, targets to set up and fireworks to prepare – I still had time to catch most of the show from the wings.

Highlights from opening night at the Zarathustra's Circus:

- The triple flip that the youngest Yang, little Zhang Li, landed to finish the Red Arrows' performance, a move that saw her land on her father's shoulders
- Atlas in tiny gold shorts, his skin shiny with oil, lifting the Krazy Kar over his head and walking off as the Krazy Klowns scrambled after him
- Eshe and Rodrigo dancing the cha-cha-cha as they flew through the air from the high trapeze
- Gladys the wonder dog nipping Gareth's magic wand out of his hand and using it to make him disappear
- Dead-Eye firing a bullet through an apple that Dmitri had placed on his head
- Kenise 'the Cat' Williams, sleek and powerful, prowling across the high wire
- A glimpse of Sadie cheering in her seat, Hussein whistling and Mum with a smile so big it could light the Big Top

That just left the fireworks.

A spotlight followed Atlas as he carried the 'launch pad' (a large safety box) and placed it in the centre of the ring. Dmitri entered next and a drumroll started. That was my cue to run on with the indoor fireworks.

Inside the launch pad were seven metal rocket stands shaped like hollow cannons, pointing upwards. I slid a Whirly Wheel into the first chute, a Comet into the second, and so on, leaving the Starburst and Showstopper for last. Once I checked the wicks were dangling from the end of each rocket, I stepped out of the way so Dmitri could light them.

It was SO exciting! Between the smell of gunpowder, the drum roll and the lone spotlight that swirled over a pitch-black Big Top, I couldn't stand still.

Finally, Dmitri lit the first wick and . . . nothing happened.

He tried again.

The wick flickered . . . and went out.

It happened again and again. None of the indoor fireworks would light.

Meanwhile, the drumroll beat and the spotlight whirled around the tent. The crowd began to do a slow handclap.

Dmitri shook the ends of the rocket again, then lit a match.

Nothing happened.

The drumroll beat. The spotlight swirled and the crowd continued to clap.

'What's wrong?' I asked.

'The rockets are soft, damp on end,' Dmitri scowled. 'Water must have gotten into box. The gunpowder will not light.'

'Let me try.' I cupped the end of the rocket stand with both hands and turned up the heat. My hands blazed orange, then red. Squeezing the end of the Whirly Wheel, I felt the rocket ignite.

Whoosh!

It shot into the air, bursting into shimmers of white and gold.

We swapped roles. Dmitri took the box of indoor fireworks and slid them into each chute and I lit them, burning through the ends of the rockets until their charge of gunpowder ignited.

Neither of us spoke, as we moved back and forth

in the launch pad, firing rockets. Because of the smoke curling around us, it was hard to see. It also, I realised, made me invisible to the crowds of spectators around us. By the time we lit the Showstopper – a burst-blast of red and gold sparkles in the shape of a bear – my face was black with soot and my ears were ringing.

Dmitri re-entered the centre ring as the last sparkles faded. The spotlight found him.

'Ladies and gentlemen, boys and girls, thank you for coming to Zarathustra's Travelling Circus. Goodnight!'

The spotlight vanished.

When the house lights came back on, I found Dmitri standing next to me

'Oi!' I shouted. 'How did you do that?'

Taking my hands, Dmitri turned them over. 'That is my line,' he grinned. 'How did *you* do that?'

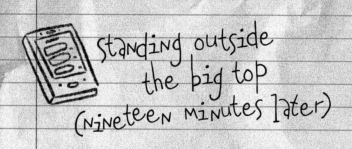

Standing outside
the big top
(Nineteen minutes later)

Sitting inside the costume caravan, I checked my phone. I had told Mum not to wait for me after the show and she had walked Sadie and Hussein home. She and Sadie had messaged me as they left. Both of them loved the circus, especially the fireworks at the end.

There were a few texts from Hussein too.

They weren't about tonight's performance. It seemed as if he had spent most of the show eavesdropping on Ash Aitkens.

A series of text messages sent from Hussein Aziz to Aidan Sweeney and Sadie Laurel-Hewitt on Friday.

At 7:35pm:
R friend opened his present this evening. Didn't get what he asked 4.
NOT a happy boy.

At 7:43pm:
Evening at Ritz ended in disaster. Scenes!

At 7:52pm:
10 calls to South America in last half-hour.

At 8:07pm:
List of possible suspects made.
It's short.
One name only: Sloane Sixsmith!

YES! WE DID IT!

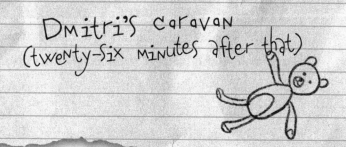

Dmitri's Caravan
(twenty-six minutes after that)

Gareth and Gladys were in Dmitri's caravan when I arrived. Both magician and collie seemed upset. Worry lines creased Gareth's forehead and Gladys lay at his feet, her ears drooping.

'I thought London would be different, Dmitri, but it's not. It's worse. Did you see the empty seats?'

Dmitri nodded. He was at his desk. The top button of his shirt was open and his bow-tie undone.

'This is it,' Gareth said. 'It's the end of the road. If we can't fill the Big Top on opening night, what chance do we have?' He jerked his thumb at me. 'We can't pin all our hopes on the Fool here. It's not fair to the lad.'

'I am working on it,' Dmitri said.

'I hope so.' Gareth took a woolly hat out of his pocket and pulled it down over his head. 'We're counting on you, Dmitri.'

Buttoning up his coat, Gareth whistled for Gladys. The collie hopped up and they walked out the door.

Once we were alone, Dmitri asked, 'What you think of first night at circus?'

'It was epic! Honestly, Dmitri. Best night ever.'

Dmitri's face broke into a smile. 'Good! This I like to hear. Better than hearing circus seats are empty.'

'Is everything allright?'

Dmitri shrugged. 'It could be better, it could be worse. Except for the fireworks tonight . . . that was very special. I was right about you and fire, eh? Even better, you give me idea. Many boys and girls want to light fireworks, right?'

'Absolutely. Watching them explode was brilliant!'

'We sell ticket – one special ticket every night,' Dmitri said, thumping his desk with excitement, his blue eyes shining. 'Light fireworks. Do roly-poly with Li Jun. Hide in magic box with Gladys. Give chance to be part of circus, not watch only from seat.'

'People would love it,' I cried. 'Everyone would love to be an acrobat or clown for one night.'

Dmitri clapped his hands. 'Good! It is settled. I will work on it tomorrow. You see, you bring circus good luck already! First, you rescue fireworks, now show me way to make money.'

'Thanks, Dmitri. You're the best!'

'This I like to hear,' Dmitri grinned. 'What about you, do you have question for me?'

'Just one.' I pointed the postcards and photographs that covered the walls of his caravan. 'Who's the bear?'

Chuckling, Dmitri got to his feet. 'That is Zarathustra.'

'Zarathustra is a bear?'

'*Russian* bear,' the old man said, pounding his chest. 'Black bear. I raise him since he was small cub. Together we travel the world. Come closer and see.'

Images of Dmitri and the black bear covered the far wall. There were hundreds of them – photos of Dmitri and Zarathustra in front of the Eiffel Tower and Taj Mahal; snapshots from outside farms and roadsides with the dates and place names printed underneath; children's drawings of a hairy ringmaster with a black bear; and one image of them both squeezed into seat of a rollercoaster. In some photos, Dmitri was young, his hair was ink-black and he was sporting an enormous moustache. In others, he was grey-haired and bearded.

'Zarathustra, my old friend.' Removing a red handkerchief from a pocket, Dmitri rubbed the dust off a photo of them in front of Big Ben. 'Forty years we spent together, here in this caravan. No wife or children for me. Just bear. Very gentle bear. Children love him. People come from all over world to see him. Zarathustra become so famous, we name circus after him.'

'You lived in *here* with a bear?'

'I did,' the old man chuckled.

'How?'

'Very carefully.' Dmitri winked.

I checked the walls and ceilings of the caravan. There were claw marks on the doorpost and paw prints on the ceiling. The springs on the sofa sagged and groaned. Two chairs had bite marks running down their legs and the small refrigerator seemed battered and beaten. I glanced nervously down the narrow hall that led to the back room of the caravan. 'Where is Zarathustra now?'

'Zarathustra had long, happy life,' Dmitri said. 'He is in heaven now.'

I glanced around his narrow caravan. 'This place must seem empty without him.'

Nodding, the old man fell silent.

I went quiet too.

Forty years!

I tried to imagine Dmitri and Zarathustra in this caravan – sitting down to tea together; driving down the M1 in the caravan, Zarathustra in the passenger seat, Dmitri driving; sharing the sofa.

Poor Dmitri.

If Lemon didn't cuddle up on my camp-bed at night, I couldn't sleep. What must it be like to miss a bear?

That got me to thinking about Mum, and Mum reminded me of Dad, and the next thing I knew, I had a lump in my throat the size of a tennis ball.

'Dmitri,' I croaked, 'I'd better go.'

'Yes, go. It is late. But take this.' Reaching into a box on the floor, Dmitri pulled out a stuffed black bear. 'I owe prize, eh?' he said, handing it to me. 'Little bear like Zarathustra. He bring smile on lonely night.'

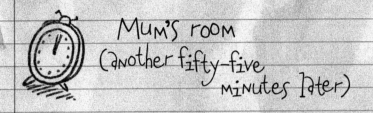

Mum's room
(another fifty-five
minutes later)

I put the bear on Mum's bed and stuck a note between his paws.

Mum,
Look what I
won just for you!
Ax

make me

The flat was empty when I got home on Sunday night. There wasn't much in the fridge, not that I was hungry. Three boxes of popcorn goes a long way.

It had been a long weekend. There were two shows each day, a matinee and an evening performance, and I was tired. Taking on an after-school job was more trouble than I had imagined. It left me feeling like I was being pulled in three directions: by school, the circus and Ash Aitkens.

This is a summary of how they were all going:

School
Homework on the weekend – what was that about? Isn't locking us up between half-eight and four all week enough? I had maths (ugh), science (project on the conduction of heat – okay, that might be

useful) *and* English (a worksheet titled 'Fun with Colons': yeah, right). Don't they know I have a *life*?

Speaking of which . . .

Zarathustra's Travelling Circus

Three days into Zarathustra's London tour and already the crowds were beginning to thin. Three rows at the back were always empty and more spaces were opening nearer the ringside. Even Saturday night, the big draw, didn't sell out and that left a few circus stars shaken. Rodrigo broke into a tango on the wrong cue and Gareth the Magician muddled his card trick again. (He should ask Gladys to do it. She's the brains in their duo.) Mathilde refuses to answer questions about Zarathustra's future, stomping away when anyone asks her how long she thinks the circus will stay open. And me . . . I can't help feeling I've left everyone down. I'm not the Fool, I'm a dud, the firecracker that wouldn't light.

Ash Aitkens

Hussein was keeping a close watch on Ash Aitkens and his texts and messages. So far, from texts, we knew: Aitkens was holed up in Essex doing little else but complaining, crying and checking news feeds from Peru. Over the internet we learned that Sloane Sixsmith was still in hospital and receiving no calls or visitors, and that Cambio Laboratories had released a report confirming their unique and irreplaceable greenhouse had been destroyed. Hussein said that Aitkens had spent Sunday morning Googling 'cheap flights to Peru'.

We were almost in the clear.

Because I was alone in the flat, it made sense to make good use of my time. Locking myself into the bathroom, I opened the window and undressed.

Lighting fireworks with my hands was fun, but it wasn't enough.

I was itching to burn.

Positioning myself in the middle of the room, I ignited gradually, letting the fire begin at the top of my head and allowing the flames to spread down my body. I lifted off the floor and hovered in the air, arms spread wide. As I floated, I could see myself burn in the mirror. Flames licked my skin in shades of red, yellow and orange. It was so ... *beautiful*. There was no other word for it.

Beautiful.

There's a word I've never used before when looking at myself in front of a mirror.

I remained in mid-air, flames leaping, burning and spinning until I heard a door slam. Dousing my flames quickly, I threw my pyjamas on.

'Mum?' I said, opening the door.

There was no answer. I walked into the sitting room.

'Mum?'

When no one answered, I ran to the sofa. Alarmed, I pulled out my suitcase and opened it.

Oh, no.

Clothes were stuffed down the sides. My wash bag had been turned inside-out. Socks were tossed left and right and my KEEP CALM shirt was nowhere to be seen.

Smoke curled out of my ears as panic gripped me.

I pulled out my football boot and found my sock where I'd left it, tucked inside the toe. I looked inside my sock.

It was empty.

I checked the boot.

Nothing.

I tried my hoodie, jumper, jeans, my spare school uniform, T-shirts and pants.

Nothing.

No! No! No! No!

How?

How had Ash Aitkens known where to find the jar of sweets?

I emptied the suitcase on the floor and tore through every item of clothing I owned. I checked under the sofa and chairs, under their cushions and down the sides. I looked in the closet and under the table. I was so frantic that the hairs on my arms were not only standing up, but smoking. There was no way I could have lost that jar! I was in such a state I began to talk aloud.

'Think! Think!' I said. 'Where could it be?'

The door to the sitting room swung open.

It was Granny.

Around me, the sitting room looked like a bomb site. Cushions up-ended, clothes scattered everywhere. I expected a tongue-lashing or worse, but she surprised me.

She chuckled. 'Looking for something?'

It took a few seconds for that to sink in.

NO! Not Granny!

'You know the rules,' Granny sneered. 'No sweets in the bed or on the sofa.'

'Granny, you can't! Please. That jar is important.'

'Rules are rules, boy.'

'You don't understand, Granny,' I cried. 'You *have* to give those sweets back!'

The hairy eyebrow arrowed downwards. Her twitchy eye skipped. Her good one fixed me with a long, cold stare.

'Make me,' she said.

call the army

'SHE DID WHAT?'

'Keep it down, Hussein,' I said, glancing over at Mulch and his mates huddling near us against the wall.

We were in the concrete court outside D Block. It was morning break, my first moment alone with Hussein since school started.

'PLEASE TELL ME YOU'RE JOKING!'

He wasn't taking the news about last night well.

Heads turned in our direction. 'Not so loud,' I said again in a low voice.

'This is a disaster!' He slumped against the wall, chin trembling. 'No offence, Aidan, but your grandmother is a psychopath.'

I preferred 'deranged', but I wasn't going to argue with him. 'No offence taken.'

'Worrying about You-Know-Who having that sort of power is bad enough, but your grandmother? Who knows what kind of monster she might turn into.'

'I know. I was up half the night worrying about it.'

Three possible supervillains Granny might turn into:

1. **The Hag of Doom**

   The Hag is a fierce, war-loving goddess of destruction. Dressed in grey battle armour, her greatest weapon is her walking stick. One blast of her 'thunder-cane' can cause ruptures in the Earth's core, shattering buildings and pulverising the pocket money of any child within a ten-mile vicinity.

2. **She-Bear**

   Half-woman, half-bear, She-Bear is a monstrous grizzly-beast. Scaling walls with her claws, she tracks down young boys for sport. Notoriously bad-tempered, She-Bear is best known for her inhuman strength, fighting skills and stinky breath.

3. Granzilla

Towering over the London skyline, Granzilla stalks the city streets, squishing schoolboys and flattening apartment blocks. Armour-plated, long-tailed and surviving on gin and peanuts, Granzilla takes no prisoners. Run away – while you can!

Hussein said, 'If your gran swallows one of those sweets, we're all in danger.'

'Danger?' I said. 'Hussein, we are talking about the future of the world here. Granny with superpowers could take civilization back to the dark ages.'

'Do you think so?'

'I live with her,' I said grimly. 'I know what I'm talking about.'

'Maybe you're right,' Hussein sighed. 'Do you think we should contact the police?'

'We need to think bigger, Hussein.'

'Bigger?'

'Lives are at stake. It's the Army we want. A few tanks, maybe a rocket launcher or two.'

Hussein stared at me. 'The Army?'

'I've given this a lot of thought.'

'Have you?' Hussein said. He held his hand up

to his mouth as if he were speaking into a phone. 'Hello, General? Aidan Sweeney here. Would you mind marching a few platoons up to Kentish Town? My granny is about to lay waste to London.'

'Tanks,' I said. 'I want tanks. There will be carnage if Granny gets super-charged. The names on Granny's hit list could run into the thousands.'

A brief list (in no particular order) of individuals, groups and/or species who, for their own safety, should consider moving abroad if Granny develops superpowers:

- The former warden of HM Rockaway Prison, Stella Blanche-Bucket
- Pigeons
- The Labour Party
- Banjo players
- Drivers and passengers on the Routemaster 134 bus
- Ash Aitkens
- ME

'We can't do that, Aidan,' Hussein said. 'The Army won't believe you until they see your grandmother's powers for themselves.'

He was right.

Scratching my chin, I pondered this momentous problem, one which risked the future safety of England, if not the world. The solution, when I arrived at it, was obvious.

'Hussein, destiny has forced our hand,' I declared. Fists clenched, chest out, jaw straight, I struck a heroic pose. 'The time has come for us to assemble.'

'Again? We had assembly this morning.'

'Not assembly, *assemble*. Like the Avengers.'

'The Avengers!' Hussein nodded.

'Working together, me, you and Sadie can defeat whatever awful monster Granny becomes.'

'What about Ash Aitkens?' Hussein checked behind him to make sure no one was eavesdropping. 'He's still out there. He's not gone away, not yet.'

'Aitkens' security team may be watching the building, but they're not inside it. If we take Granny on indoors, they'll never know.'

Hussein considered my proposal. 'We could wear disguises. No one would recognise us that way, including your granny.'

'What kind of disguises?'

Hussein blushed. 'I don't know. Something with a cape.'

'Go superhero on her? Computo and Fire Boy to the rescue?' I shook my head. 'I don't think so, mate. If you and I showed up wearing masks and tights, I'm pretty sure Granny would know it was us.'

'You think so?'

'Yeah. Don't let that twitchy eye fool you. She doesn't miss a thing.'

'I guess you're right.'

Fists clenched, chest out, jaw straight, I struck another heroic pose. 'If I'm going to stare death in the face, I'll do it as Aidan Sweeney.'

'Agreed,' Hussein said. He swaggered forward. 'Own clothes it is.'

'Street life.'

We bumped fists. 'Keeping it real.'

'Keeping what real, Sweeney?' Mulch sneered, his cronies circling around him. 'Your belt, I hope. The last thing I want to see again is your bum.'

I shoved him aside and walked away. There were far more important foes for me to face than Mitchell Mulch.

'C'mon, Hussein. We've got a world to save.'

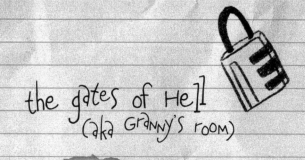

the gates of Hell
(aka GRANNY'S rOOM)

I checked my watch.

'The afternoon All-You-Can-Eat special at Bobo's Grill is officially closed. I reckon we have ten minutes to find the jar of Nature's Own before Granny gets back – assuming, that is, that she hasn't already developed some freakish superpower and will return faster.'

Hussein studied the image on his phone – he had hacked into the apartment block's CCTV camera feed.

'Lobby's clear,' he said.

Sadie tapped the notice on Granny's door. 'I wonder who this is directed at?'

NO TRESPASSING
VIOLATORS WILL BE
PROSECUTED AND PUNISHED
ESPECIALLY PRYING LITTLE BOYS

'It's like my own private entrance to Mount Doom at the end of the hall,' I said.

Hussein said, 'So how do we get in? Burn a hole through the lock?'

'That won't be necessary,' Sadie said.

Holding up her palm, she closed her eyes.

The spring coiled.

The bolt clicked.

The door swung open.

I had not entered my old bedroom since that awful day three years ago when Granny had moved into our flat. The Happy Acres Retirement Home had kicked her out for bad behaviour. (A nurse had confiscated Granny's secret stash of gin and cigars on 'doctor's orders', which had resulted in a small uprising, the riot police being called and a chase through the streets of Dagenham featuring two wheelchairs, a mobility scooter, a stolen golf cart and a restraining order.) It was only temporary, I was told. Mum had assured me that she would find Granny another home. I decamped to the sitting room and there I stayed. No retirement home in the UK would have her.

Looking around at my old room, it was as if I

had never lived here. Every trace of my old life had been removed.

The stacks of comics? Gone. My books and games? Gone. The cork board where I kept photos of Lemon, Mum, Sadie, Hussein and Dad? Gone. My ticket stubs and souvenirs, the Arsenal scarf tacked to the ceiling, my 'You're Special!' medal for coming 8th in the All Hallows Primary School Sports Day race? Gone, all of them.

And what was there instead?

A list of items found during a preliminary search of Flat 3D's corner room, aka 'Granny's room':

– A wall-to-wall widescreen plasma TV
– A Bristle tournament-style dartboard (worn)
– Two bottles of Guzzler's Gin (emptied)
– A set of dumb-bells
– One brown-leather La-Z-Boy chair
– A collection of forest animals sculpted from barbed wire
– Trophies, medals and rosettes in activities such as darts and arm-wrestling
– A collection of Bavarian Beer Festival beer mats

- One ash-tray (overflowing)
- The September edition of *Combat* magazine
- One storage trunk (black)

The black trunk, long and deep and wide, occupied one corner of the room. Steel edging ran along its sides and a thick padlock hung from its lid.

You could fit a lot of barbed-wire forest creatures in there.

Or worse.

'I can't open a padlock,' Sadie said.

'It's a combination lock,' said Hussein. 'My powers won't work on it either.'

'What will we do?' I cried. 'I can't burn it off. She'll blame me. I know she will.'

'Don't panic,' Sadie said. 'It's only a three-digit lock. That shouldn't be hard to break.'

'Try its factory settings, 0-0-0,' Hussein said. 'Most people don't change it.'

Sadie spun the dials.

It didn't work. Neither did 9-9-9, 1-2-3, 3-2-1 or 7-7-7.

And then Hussein glimpsed a large old woman

with a walking stick pushing her way through the lobby doors on his feed.

'SHE'S COMING!' he cried.

Flames burst out of my head. Smoke mushroomed out of my bottom. I didn't know whether I was up or down.

'Calm down,' Sadie said. 'Hussein, when she gets into the lift, use your powers to halt it. Keep her stuck between floors until we open this.' She rubbed her chin. 'Think! It must be three numbers important to her. When's her birthday?'

'SHE'S TAKING THE STAIRS!'

'The 22nd of January.' I glanced nervously at the door. 'Come on, Sadie. Leave it.'

'What about your mum's birthday?'

'The 3rd of November,' I whimpered.

'No, that's not it.'

'SHE'S ON THE FIRST FLOOR!'

'Come on, Sadie,' I cried, hopping about as flames rocketed out of my ears.

'Just want to try one more ... Got it.' The padlock snapped open. Sadie unhooked its shackle and opened the trunk.

The jar of Nature's Own was on top.

Underneath, in neatly stacked piles, were my comics, my medals, my books and board-games, the photos of me and my friends, and even stuff I had forgotten: school certificates, football stickers, scarfs and mittens, notebooks and much more.

Sadie and I stared down into the trunk. 'It was 2-4-5 that opened the lock,' she said softly.

2-4-5.

The 24th of May was my birthday.

'SECOND FLOOR!'

I threw the jar to Hussein. While I waved away the smoke, Sadie closed the trunk and locked it. By the time Granny burst through the door, Hussein and I were propped up in front of the TV playing *FIFA* and Sadie was sprawled on the floor with Lemon.

What a team.

And BEST of all, we had checked the jar and Granny hadn't eaten a single sweet.

The world could breathe easily again.

the storeroom

No one wanted a repeat of that close call. The last drops of *el Árbol de los Dioses* were far too precious to hide away in a sock. I needed a more secure location.

Luckily, I knew just the place.

The circus had one caravan which doubled as a storeroom. It housed costumes, props, clown suits, fancy hats, winter outfits and more. It also contained a row of padlocked lockers which were hidden behind a clothes rack and bolted to the floor. When I joined the circus, Dmitri had told me to use this storeroom whenever I changed into my circus kit (a maroon T-shirt with a bear in a circus hat on the back and *Zarathustra's Travelling Circus* written in gold letters across the front).

Opening a locker, I placed the jar of Nature's

Own inside and padlocked it shut.

Good luck finding that, Granny.

'You 'ave sweet tooth, eh?'

Startled, I somersaulted over the locker and fell into a tub stuffed with silk scarfs and old costumes. Fighting free of a pink tutu, I got to my feet.

It was Mathilde. She wore a ripped leather jacket and a red velvet hat. In her hands were two necklaces, one a metal chain as thick as a bike lock and the other a string of shark teeth. Standing in front of a full-length mirror, she held each up and studied her image.

'Do you always 'ide your sweeties?'

'No,' I said, picking a strand of pink fluff from my shirt.

Mathilde caught my eye in the mirror. 'Even your special sweeties?'

I dropped the tutu and stared at her.

'Don't worry,' she said, noting my expression. 'I do not want zem.' Leaning into her reflection, she checked her black lipstick and arched an eyebrow at me. 'I 'ave a date tonight. If Dmitri asks, say nothing.'

'Why?'

Mathilde put down the shark teeth. ''Ee zink I am still little girl.' She looped the chain necklace over her head and adjusted it over her chest. 'I am not little girl.'

I said, 'You look pretty grown up to me.'

Mathilde threw her head back, posing like a celebrity in front of a row of cameras. I laughed.

She swapped hats, putting the red velvet one aside and trying on a leather skull-cap that looked like an ancient helmet. 'Zis caravan was my favourite place when I was young. In 'ere, I play dress-up. Queen one day. King zee next.'

Kneeling, I collected the scarves I'd knocked over. 'What was it like growing up in a circus?'

'I know nothing else but zee circus.' She shrugged. 'Always on zee move.'

'What was Zarathustra like, Dmitri's bear?'

'Zarathustra?' Mathilde smiled at my reflection in the mirror. 'Zarathustra was zee best. I would climb his back every day and 'old 'is ears. "Run! Run!" I'd shout.' She pulled an ancient ringmaster's coat off a hanger and sniffed its sleeve. 'I can still smell him.'

'I always wanted to go camping with a bear. Climb trees together. Watch him fish.'

Mathilde sighed. '*Oui*. It is not zee same since 'ee passed. Without Zarathustra zee bear, zere is a big 'ole in our circus.' She fluffed up her hair, pouted once more into the mirror, and went out.

A tiny buzz from my pocket woke me from my bear dreams. I took my phone out and read the text.

It was good news.

VERY good news.

A text message sent from Hussein Aziz to Aidan Sweeney and Sadie Laurel-Hewitt on Monday at 6:17pm:
AA HAS BOUGHT TICKET TO PERU!!!
FLIGHT LEAVES TOMORROW MORNING!

Everything was going to plan. Once Ash Aitkens boarded his flight, we would be safe. And Hussein could place every one of his files into the hands of the police. They would have all the evidence they needed.

Happy days!

By this time tomorrow, I would be burning bright and flying high!

circus school

The next day, Dmitri asked the circus stars and their families to gather in front of his caravan before the evening performance.

He appeared on the steps of his caravan half-dressed, with the braces of his ringmaster outfit slung over a vest. Three dark worry lines dug into his forehead and his grey-white hair needed combing. He placed two fingers into his mouth and gave a long, shrill whistle. The chattering stopped.

'I will not beat bush. Our circus is in trouble. You see the crowds. Zarathustra's comes to London, great city of the world, but London does not come to our circus.' Rubbing his whiskery cheeks, Dmitri pawed the ground with his boot. 'Times have changed. It is different world now, not like long ago.'

'Jamaica is warm this time of year, Dmitri,' Kenise Williams called out. 'Let's go there!'

A few chuckled.

'I say we try Paris!'

'Amsterdam!'

'Merthyr Tydfil!'

Dmitri sighed. 'Yes. This was always the way. If no crowd, we leave. Pack tent. Hitch caravans. Go. Move to next town. But not now.' He waved a hand at the grass and the Big Top beyond. 'Now, we pay drivers first. Pay rent. Pay city.' His jowls sagged and the bags under his eyes swelled. 'We cannot go on like this.'

Rodrigo buried his face into his hands and sobbed.

'Hellfire!' drawled Dead-Eye. 'It looks like this is the last corral.'

Li Jun Yang croaked, 'No one wants to see us any more.'

Gladys the wonder dog howled.

The only person who didn't seem upset was Mathilde. Still wearing the leather skull-cap and jacket, she stared straight at Dmitri, her face blank and looking as if she hadn't a care in the world.

This, I found reassuring.

Dmitri whistled again, and the crowd fell silent.

'Wait, please. I did not finish. Times change. So must circus. We either fill Big Top to keep circus open . . . or we find other way to make money. I have other way. I call it, "Circus School".'

For the next ten minutes, Dmitri explained his idea, one he credited me for giving him. Basically, Circus School meant giving boys and girls a chance to be a clown or acrobat with Zarathustra's Circus for one day. There wouldn't be classes for now, only one-to-one sessions taught by the circus stars themselves. And then, as a special treat, the boys and girls would appear in an actual performance, lining up alongside their performer and showing the crowd what they learned.

Some of the circus stars were delighted.

'I always wanted to teach rope-walking,' Kenise said.

Li Jun Yang agreed. 'What is another gymnast to the Red Arrows? They need only get in line.'

Others weren't so happy.

'School? Hellfire!' drawled Dead-Eye. 'I ain't goin' back there, Dmitri! I joined the circus to get out of school!'

Gareth agreed with Dead-Eye. 'I'm sorry, Dmitri,

but I share Gladys with no one.'

Dmitri listened to their concerns, but told them Circus School seemed the only way to keep their circus rolling onwards. 'I even sold first ticket for Circus School to schoolboy today. He will perform at tonight's show.'

The crowd gasped.

'Tonight?'

'So soon?'

'When did you plan on telling us?'

'It is boy's birthday and he wants to be ringmaster, so tonight he will be me. We let him strut in spotlight and smile and wave.'

'What is he like?' Eshe asked.

'More trouble than wolf at picnic,' Dmitri said with a weary shake of his head. 'But it must be done. One place at Circus School is same price as four *rows* of seats. Think of that! This boy makes crowd bigger too. His friends come with boy's father to see young ringmaster. This is how we keep Zarathustra's moving forward – as school and circus!'

Everyone clapped.

'Three cheers for Dmitri!' someone shouted at the back.

Dmitri held up a hand. 'Do not thank me, thank Aidan too. Without him, we have no Circus School.'

People clapped. Eshe kissed the top of my head and Atlas threw me up into the air.

Dmitri grinned and called the meeting to an end with a promise to give every person in the audience a circus show they will never forget.

We bounced away with a spring in our step. It seemed like Zarathustra's Travelling Circus might carry on for years and years now!

Or at least, that's what we thought.

the ringmaster

It was nearly showtime that night when Atlas stopped me outside the Big Top.

'Fool!' he boomed. 'Have you seen Dmitri?'

I hadn't.

'He is needed. Go find Dmitri and tell him that I, Atlas, have asked for him.'

I trotted past the stalls to the rear of the grounds where the caravans were parked. I hadn't gone far when I heard two voices. One belonged to a boy and the other to a loud, rude man.

'Daddy!' the boy said. 'Tell him! Tell the nasty man! He won't listen to me!'

'You heard the boy, Dmitri,' the man answered. 'If my son wants a whip, he gets a whip.'

My heart sank. I recognised the boy's voice. His needling, nasty whine was hard to mistake. It was Mitchell Mulch.

Not wanting to be seen by Mulch or his father, I crawled under Dmitri's caravan and hid.

A moment later, Mulch, kitted out in a ringmaster's costume, swaggered out of the caravan and cracked his whip.

Slash! Off came the heads of three climbing roses.

Snap! The corner of Dmitri's caravan splintered and chipped.

Slit! The tyre on a unicycle burst.

Descending the steps of the caravan with Dmitri was Mulch's father. 'Look at my boy!' his father beamed. 'He's a natural!'

Hat pushed back on his head, a button undone on his vest, shirt-tail sticking out over his trousers, Dmitri seemed frazzled. He grabbed hold of Mulch's whip. 'Use this only when no one is near. Young boys and girls are in crowd. Is dangerous. Understand?'

'Give me that!' Mulch cried, snatching his whip back. He pulled the top hat down on to his head and straightened his bow-tie. 'My friends are waiting for me.'

'First, we go over programme,' Dmitri said.

'I *said*, I want to see my friends,' Mulch cried, stamping his foot.

'Let the boy see his mates, Dmitri,' boomed Mulch's father. 'I did pay for twenty seats remember, on top of this Circus School ticket. I'm expecting to get my money's worth, do you hear me?'

'Go,' Dmitri said to Mulch. 'Meet me at performers' entrance before curtain raises. You will hear announcement.'

Mulch cracked his whip again, scattering a pile of fallen leaves, and walked towards the Big Top with his father. As soon as the two of them rounded the caravans, Dmitri said, 'Aidan. You can come out now.'

I crawled of the shadows and brushed the dirt off my trousers.

Dmitri sighed. He jerked his thumb in Mulch's direction. 'You know this boy?'

'Too well.'

The hairs on Dmitri's chest and forearms bristled. 'I do not trust him.'

'I don't blame you.'

Dmitri laid a wide hand on my shoulder. 'Be careful. He wants to make trouble for you.'

I was not surprised.

'You and Atlas,' Dmitri continued. 'He wants one of you on each side, following him around the ring like monkeys. Jump when he say "Jump". Kneel when he say "Kneel". I tell him this is wrong. This is not what ringmaster do. But boy and father, they do not care.'

'Dmitri, I'm sorry, but there is NO WAY I am kneeling to Mitchell Mulch.'

'Do not worry. Atlas will follow boy about. He likes spotlight. He will flex and pose.' Dmitri scratched his chin. 'But you must stay away. When birthday boy enters ring, go to wings. When he is in wings, go to rear. I will keep bad apple moving. Tonight, no fireworks.' Dmitri stopped and studied my face. 'This sound good?'

No, it didn't.

I didn't like it one bit.

But I didn't say that though. I promised Dmitri I'd stay out of the way and let someone else light the indoor fireworks.

'Good boy,' Dmitri said, with a grin. 'You shall see. It will be great show tonight. I feel it in my bones.'

big top, big trouble

Dmitri gave a signal and – Boom! Rat-a-tat! Boom! – drums thumped. Horns tooted. The curtains opened and the circus stars entered the Big Top. The performers made a ring around Dmitri and the lights dimmed.

A narrow spotlight shone on the entrance.

'Ladies and gentlemen, boys and girls, for tonight, and tonight only,' Dmitri said into the microphone, 'Zarathustra's Travelling Circus has a special guest. A *new* ringmaster. A *young* ringmaster who is twelve years old today. Please welcome . . . Mitchell Mulch!'

Mulch swanned out into the spotlight, whip in hand and waving his top hat at the crowd. Three times he pranced around the centre ring, skipping about like a fool and blowing kisses to the crowd. On each circuit, he stopped in front of the VIP seats where his parents were sat, along with Joe Jackson and most of my class from school. Mulch spent ages with them, taking no notice of the crowd or waiting performers. By the time he rejoined Dmitri after the third loop, the crowd was bored and the circus stars were furious. Kenise stood, arms folded, stamping her foot; little Zhang Li Yang was in knots; and Dead-Eye's right eye had begun twitching – *not* a good sign.

It went downhill fast from there.

When the Red Arrows raced on to tumble and spin, Mulch cracked his whip. This startled Grandpa Yang who had been standing on the shoulders of his son, Li Jun. Grandpa Yang tottered and the seven Red Arrows fell. Little Zhang Li left the ring in tears. Mulch laughed.

During Atlas's act, Mulch insisted that Atlas hold him sitting on a throne in his right arm and lift everything else with his left.

He used the microphone to blow raspberries at Eshe and Rodrigo.

He called Gareth the magician 'weird' and Gladys a show-off.

He told the circus band they were 'boring'.

He said Dead-Eye was a 'loser'. When she stomped off, after refusing to shoot holes through the canvas of the Big Top like he asked, Mulch booed. The rest of the crowd watched in silence.

Mulch couldn't get enough of the Krazy Klowns though. He giggled when Donal mowed his brothers down with the Krazy Kar. He roared when Finbar chased Shane with a giant sledge-hammer. He chuckled and chortled when Shane fought back with a flame-thrower.

Poor Dimitri. He chased after Mulch, but the boy was like a loose ferret. There was no stopping him. At this rate, it wouldn't surprise me if Circus School closed its doors after just one day. In fact, it seemed as if the only person who had escaped the Mulch treatment was me. Not trusting Dmitri's idea of staying hidden in the wings or the rear of the Big Top, I had decided to spend the night inside the vaulting box.

The vaulting box was a hollow, flat-topped box at the edge of the ring. The Red Arrows somersaulted across it; Gladys the wonder dog jumped over it; Kenise danced on it; and Shane often threatened to chain-saw it and his brothers in two. Painted red and gold, it had a latch-door on one side for props and equipment. I often spent a part of each performance inside this box looking out through its spy-holes, waiting to collect props or put them out whenever the lights went down. Now, with Mulch prowling the wings, it was easier to stay inside the vaulting box for the entire show.

The Krazy Klowns sped through their last appearance as if they were determined to get it over in a hurry. Ignoring Mulch, they screeched to a halt in the centre of the stage in their Krazy Kar. Shane pulled funny faces and squirted bubbles while Donal set fire to his brothers' trousers as if he had somewhere else to be. One quick bow later, they headed for the exits.

Mulch raced after them. 'Hey! Where do you think you're going?' he whined. 'I want to play!'

Finbar lifted himself out of a tub of water and wrung out his trousers. 'Go suck an egg.'

'What did you say?'

'You heard me.'

Mulch stamped his foot. 'You can't talk to me like that. I'm the ringmaster!'

'Oh, the *ringmaster*! Excuse me!' Turning, he

wiggled his bottom at Mulch. The trumpet player in the circus band joined in, blasting out the longest fart sound ever. Every time you thought it had finished, Finbar squeezed out a little more. Shane and Donal joined in, holding their noses and pointing at Finbar's bottom as if it were a mad, malfunctioning machine.

The crowd laughed and laughed.

'Stop that!' Mulch shouted. 'This isn't funny!'

The Kerrigan brothers stuck their tongues out and did a silly dance around him.

Mulch was furious. 'Listen to me! When I say stop, you *stop*!' Mulch cracked his whip – and caught the three of them on the back of the legs.

The Krazy Klowns stopped dancing.

Hitching up their polka-dot trousers, they marched towards Mulch. Big grins may have been painted across their mouths and cheeks, but there were now three fierce scowls underneath.

Tips on how to get along with others #3:
Clowns can be good friends or cruel, unforgiving enemies. Choose wisely.

It became an all-out clown attack. From ping-pong balls and fish-slaps to exploding sunflowers and rude gestures, Mulch got bombarded. The brothers stuffed a rubber chicken down his trousers, punched a hole through his top hat and cut the tail off his ringmaster's costume. The circus band joined in, adding a jolly tune to each kick, bop or pull. Mulch didn't know where to turn.

Everyone roared with laughter – apart from Mulch's parents, that is.

Alone in the centre ring, covered in flour and glitter, Mulch fumed, cracking his whip again and again, splintering the tub, cutting notches in the centre pole and puncturing a tall tin can in a cage marked 'Safety Zone'.

The can toppled over. Inside it was the lighter fluid for the flame-thrower. The fluid spilt, trickling towards me and pooling around the sides of the vaulting box.

Was I alarmed?

A little. Lighter fluid was dangerous. But as long as Mulch didn't pick up the flame-thrower, it wasn't a problem.

Mulch picked up the flame-thrower.

'You've spoilt my party,' he sobbed, tripping over the rubber chicken, which had fallen out of his trousers.

Thinking his pratfall was part of the act, the crowd laughed.

'IT'S NOT FUNNY!' he screamed.

The crowd laughed harder.

I could see Dmitri, Atlas and the Krazy Klowns circling Mulch. They must have seen the lighter fluid on the ground.

Mulch shifted the flame-thrower on to his shoulder and aimed it at the rubber chicken. 'Here's what I think of this circus.'

Staying hidden was the least of my worries now. 'Mulch!' I shouted from inside the box. 'Don't pull that trigger!'

Mulch stopped. His jaw fell open. 'Sweeney? Where *are* you?'

He dropped the flame-thrower.

When it hit the ground, it bounced. Fire sprayed out, igniting the lighter fluid and ... *whoosh!* The black puddle of liquid seeping into the vaulting box erupted into flames.

hot stuff

At some point after I developed the power to burn, I'd also noticed my sense of smell had changed.

There was a time when brownies baking in the oven had been my favourite smell. Now it was burnt toast. Bacon frying in the pan? No, thanks. Give me a whiff of petrol or engine oil instead.

So, when the lighter fluid leaked into the vaulting box, I wallowed in its balmy perfume. I sprinkled it on, dabbing drops on my wrist and behind my ears, like Mum does with L'Amour before a night out, and even added a dash more under each armpit. Yes, I knew Vulcan Premium Lighter Fluid advised against this – those large-lettered warnings with the skull and crossbones on the back of the can are hard to miss – but I couldn't help myself. To me, its gorgeous, gassy scent smelled like a summer breeze on a sunlit morning.

Needless to say, when the flames hit the vaulting box, I went up like a rocket. Fire burst from each of my limbs. Flames blazed from my chest, torching my circus-boy kit and scorching my shoes. The heat shattered the vaulting box, hurling its planks in various directions.

I stood.

I had forgotten how good – how *right* – it felt to be this hot. All those days and nights of holding my powers in, smothering my flames, fighting the urge to burn because I was afraid I might hurt someone – those were over. Power surged through my arms and chest, power like I had never experienced before. The heat was incredible. I was far, far hotter than I had ever been before.

I began to climb into the air.

I rose steadily at first, then more quickly.

Pointing my arm at the high trapeze, I exploded, zooming to the top of the circus tent and rounding the high platforms, jetting out over the centre ring.

I WAS FLYING . . . and it felt *good*!

I swooped.

I climbed.

I somersaulted.

I dived.

I made flaming loop-the-loops high above the centre ring.

When I finally descended, I landed beside the first-aid area, where the fire blanket was kept. Whipping it off its peg, keeping my back to the audience, I covered myself, the blanket pulled over my head so no one could see my face and began to race to the exit.

I didn't get far.

Five steps in, I stopped. Something was wrong. The Big Top was so quiet that the only sound I could hear was the slap of my own feet on the ground. Sticking my head out of the blanket, I looked out and discovered why.

There was only one person in the circus tent.

Me.

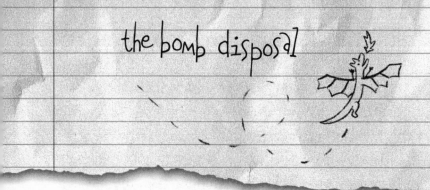

the bomb disposal

From behind the curtain of the main exit, I peeked outside. Police cars were parked near the carousel, their blue lights flashing. Officers in high-vis yellow jackets stood in front of the circus tent, shepherding people away.

'Move back, please. Move back,' a police officer shouted. 'We need to seal off the area.'

An old woman in the crowd called out to the officer. 'Have you found that . . . *thing*?'

'I nearly wet myself when that flaming dwarf rose into the air,' the man next to her said.

'It wasn't a dwarf,' a small boy said. 'It was a baby dragon.'

'You're all wrong,' an old man cried, shaking his fist. 'It was a red demon with horns and a pitchfork!'

'All we know for sure,' the police officer said, 'is that an incendiary device exploded inside the circus tent. Bomb disposal will conduct a preliminary search shortly, which is why we have been asked to clear the area. For your own safety, please, go home. The show's over.'

Bomb disposal? I didn't wait to hear any more.

At the opposite end of the Big Top, there was a loose tent flap, a hidden opening that circus performers could use to make a 'surprise' entrance or exit. I raced to it now, slipping out when I was certain no one was looking, and ran the long way round to the costumes. When I reached the storeroom, I ditched the fire blanket, threw my clothes on in the dark, and found a pair of boots in the costume box that fit me.

I peered through the window and spotted Eshe and Rodrigo, the Kerrigan brothers and Mathilde. Still in their costumes, they were gathered around the bomb disposal van. I was tempted to join them – the chance to see a bomb-disposal robot in action didn't come along often. But then again, seeing that I was the bomb they were looking for, that didn't seem like such a wise idea. I nipped quietly out of the door instead and out the back exit of the circus. When I reached the footpath, I broke into a jog.

I didn't stop running until I reached the bottom of Parliament Hill.

The moon was huge overhead, so low and round that it seemed to brush the branches of the trees. I almost felt like singing. So much had happened today! I wanted to close my eyes and re-live every second of it in my head.

I FLEW!

It was the greatest, most spectacular thing that I had ever done.

As I rounded the fields, my phone pinged. Opening it, I found ten unanswered messages.

A list of text messages sent from Hussein Aziz to Aidan Sweeney between 8:26pm and 8:42pm:
are u crazy?

there are vids of u all over the internet!!!

police are looking 4 'an unidentified flying object which is on fire and may be dangerous. residents r advised 2 stay indoors'. flying and on fire. hmmm . . . who might that be?

u promised not 2 draw attention! what do u call this?!

THIS IS NOT WHAT WE AGREED. LOW PROFILE, REMEMBER?!! a maniac is on the loose – remember him? he is on his way!! now is not the time 2 fire up!!!

what u thinking? u r going 2 ruin it for all of us!!

A list of text messages sent from Mum to Aidan Sweeney between 8:36pm and 8:47pm:
Hi, Aidan. The BBC says the police were called out to the circus this evening. Are you okay? Mum x

Hi, Aidan. Mum again. The BBC are now saying it's they've called bomb disposal! Please text. I just want to hear that you're safe. xx

WHERE ARE YOU?

A text message sent from Sadie Laurel-Hewitt to Aidan Sweeney at 8:44pm:
Hot tonight? lol

A text message sent from Aidan Sweeney to Mum at 8:49pm:
I'm fine. Nothing to worry about. Have to stay late, but will explain when I get home.

A text message sent from Aidan Sweeney to Hussein Aziz and Sadie Laurel-Hewitt at 8:50pm:
Can we meet? Must talk.

A text message sent from Sadie Laurel-Hewitt to Aidan Sweeney and Hussein Aziz at 8:51pm:
My place. :)

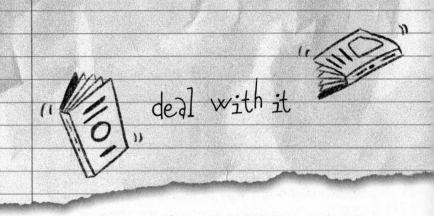

deal with it

Sadie was in her tiger onesie when she opened the door.

'Hello, Fire Boy. Everyone's talking about you.'

'You're not funny,' I grumbled, following her into the flat.

'You're the main story on BBC London.' Sadie lowered her voice so she sounded like a TV presenter. *'Witnesses claim a fiery demon invaded a circus show in North London this evening.'*

'Ha, ha.'

She led me to the study. Hussein was already there, curled on the floor, one eye on his phone.

Entering Sadie's study was like stepping into a librarian's dream. It had panelled shelves stacked with books along three walls, old maps and prints pinned up along the fourth, two leather reading chairs, an iron fireplace with rose tiles and a huge oak desk topped with a reading lamp. It's where Sadie did her homework most nights.

I collapsed into the first chair I saw.

'So, tell us,' Sadie said. 'What happened?'

I told them everything, pointing out at great length how Mulch was at fault and I was nothing but an innocent bystander.

'What's done is done,' I said finally. 'The question now is, what do we do next?'

Hussein said, 'We keep our heads down. Aitkens had a security team trailing you and your mum for a week. He must know about the circus. All we can do is hope he doesn't see the TV reports tonight.'

Sadie said, 'I hope he sees it. I want it out in the open.'

Hussein stared at her. 'Are you serious?'

'Yes. I'm tired of hiding, I'm fed up with concealing who I am and what I can do.' Sadie stretched her arms wide over her head. As she did, the furniture around us slowly rose into the air. 'It's easy for you, Hussein. Every time you log on, you can tap into your power. I can't, and neither can Aidan.'

Sadie clenched her fists. The furniture and books

began to spin around us. It was like sitting inside the eye of a tornado.

'Don't you see, Hussein? These powers are *us*. It's who we are. You developing a computer power, me controlling objects and Aidan becoming a boy on fire isn't random. Don't you remember what Sloane wrote? The serum inside those capsules adapts to each person's unique genetic coding and enhances it. So why fight it?' Sadie opened one hand wide. The books and furniture stopped in mid-air. '*This* is me, so deal with it. I am tired of bottling up who I am. If Ash Aitkens wants a fight, I say we take him on.'

'B-b-but . . .' Hussein stammered. 'We're only kids!'

'So?' Sadie sniffed. 'He's just a man.'

Hussein put down his phone. 'You don't know him like I do. You don't read all of his texts, only the ones I share with you. Ash Aitkens is mad and ruthless. He will kill whoever stands in his way. I've read what he says to his friends.' Hussein lowered his head and shuddered. 'I hate to think what he'll do to his enemies.'

'What *he'll* do?' Sadie said. 'What about us?'

Everything in the room began to vibrate – the

books on the shelves, the oak desk, the chair I was sitting in. It was like we were at the centre of a massive earthquake. We shook so much I feared the walls might crumble and crack.

'SADIE!'

It was Mimi shouting from a far-away room.

'WHAT ARE YOU DOING?'

Sadie lowered her hand. The vibrating stopped and all the furniture and books crashed to the ground.

Hussein crawled out from under the desk. 'Is it safe to come out?' he mouthed at me.

I shrugged. It was hard to say.

The study was a right mess. Books had fallen down. A lamp was on the floor. Prints and maps hung at odd angles and my chair – with me still clinging to it – had one leg in the fireplace.

'Do you want a hand tidying up?' I asked Sadie.

'No,' Sadie said with a wave of her fingers. 'I can do it myself.'

She meant it. It was as if time had gone into reverse. Books flew back to their shelves; lamps swivelled into place; the rug straightened; my chair slid back to where it belonged, dragging me along with it. In no time at all, everything was back in place.

'Damn,' Hussein said, watching from under the desk. 'I wish I could do that.'

Mr Demon

We had English for lesson one the next morning, though you wouldn't know it. We spent most of the lesson watching videos.

Of me.

Miss Spatchcock clicked the replay icon on her iPad screen. 'Fine, but this is the last time.'

A shaky, hand-held video appeared on the interactive white board. It showed a boy – me – rising out of a flaming box. Despite the flames, you could make out the fiery outline of my head, chest, arms and legs. You could see Mulch fainting as I flew and Dmitri carrying him away. You could hear the gasps from the crowd too, their screams when I spun and twirled over their heads like a small boy-sized comet.

The video was Joe Jackson's. He'd posted it on YouTube this morning after taking it on his phone last night. 'Demon Terrorises Circus', he called it. Not great, but better than 'Dwarf on Fire' or 'Little Dragon Does a Loop-the-loop'. It had over two thousand hits already.

'This video is going to make me a mint, Miss,' Joe said, rubbing his hands. 'Pictures of this fiery freak are on the cover of every tabloid and my clip is the best one out there. You wait and see. By the end of the day, it will be trending.'

'Poor Mitchell,' Miss Spatchcock said, putting down her iPad and switching off the whiteboard.

Hah!

'If you speak with him, Joseph, please tell him we hope he's better.'

As if.

Mr Henderson had told us at assembly that Mulch would not be returning to school until after half-term. He was 'recuperating' in Tenerife after his 'terrible shock'. He'd flown out this morning with his mum and dad. Apparently, Mulch needed sunshine and blue skies to get over the 'horrors' of last night.

Everyone was talking about last night. Mulch's mates, the whole gang of them, wouldn't shut up about it. Caversham was even offering counselling to those students 'traumatised by last night's events'. If ever there was a list that I deserved to be at the top of, it was that one, but I found it easier to say I wasn't at the circus that night. There was no need to draw any more attention to myself, though Jackson, for one, felt sorry for me.

'Sweeney, were you born under a bad sign?' he said. 'You put a shift in at that circus all week and the one night it kicks off, you're not there, you poor sod. Disgusted or what?'

'Gutted.'

'At least you get tonight off.'

'I do?'

'Haven't you heard? The police have closed the circus to carry out their investigation.'

That was worrying. Money was tight enough. Could the circus survive long without ticket sales? It was already struggling to make ends meet. Guilt knotted inside me. The circus wasn't just a job. For Dmitri, Mathilde, Atlas and the others, it was their home . . . their lives.

And I had let them down.

Jackson slapped me on the shoulder. 'Listen, Sweeney,' he whispered, cupping a hand to the side of his mouth, 'if you spot this fiery freak at the circus again, text me. I'll make it worth your while.'

'Sure.'

Would Jackson laugh if I told him the 'demon' was sitting next to him?

Would he whip out his phone and film me?

To be honest, I didn't care any more.

Sadie was right. I was tired of bottling up who I was.

My days of running away were over. If Ash Aitkens wanted me, then bring it on. I was ready. I'd fight fire with fire, and we'd see who came out on top.

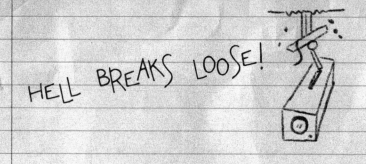

HELL BREAKS LOOSE!

Hussein and I were at the school gates after school when a black cab pulled up in front of us. A door swung open.

'Hop in,' Sadie said, sleek as ever in her Lady Pandora's blazer and boater.

A chorus of whistles and taunts accompanied us as we piled in next to her, courtesy of our fellow students.

'Charming lot, your classmates,' Sadie grinned.

'You should see them up close,' I said, kneeling on the seat and gesturing out of the back window at them for all I was worth. 'They ought to come with health warnings.'

'Enter at own risk,' Hussein suggested as the cab zoomed off.

'I was thinking more along the lines of "Beware of hazardous waste".'

The lift home had been Sadie's idea. She thought

the three of us should stay together in case Ash Aitkens swooped out of the sky to pick one of us off (me). Not that I was complaining. I could get used to travelling home from school like this. Even better, it was like old times, chatting and joking with Sadie and Hussein, swapping vids of fighting Jedi masters (Hussein) and golden retrievers bounding through fields (Sadie).

That came to an end when the cab stopped.

Five clues warning Aidan Sweeney, Sadie Laurel-Hewitt and Hussein Aziz that all was not well inside Alexandria Apartments:

1. The lobby door to Alexandria Apartments was kicked in
2. The CCTV camera guarding the entrance was wrenched away from the ceiling
3. Bits of glass were scattered across the footpath
4. A police car was parked on the forecourt
5. Curtains were blowing in the wind through a broken window on the third floor

Sadie stared up at the gaping window. 'That looks like your flat.'

'That *is* my flat.'

We slipped through the crowd gathered near the front of the building, under the police tape, and legged it up the stairs. Like the entrance to the building, our flat door was smashed in, its lock splintered and broken.

Inside, everything was a mess. Sofa cushions were sliced open and ripped apart. My suitcase was emptied out. Clothes, comics, football boots and bags were flung across the room, the bookshelf emptied.

I checked the bedrooms.

In Mum's room, Dad's photo was face-down on the floor, its frame shattered. I found the music box on the floor as well, its case cracked. No sound played and the little drummer boy had been snapped off. Heaps of clothes, torn and shredded, puddled outside the door. Prints were stripped off the walls, floorboards kicked in. It was as if someone had been looking for buried treasure and hadn't found it.

They had, however, left me a note.

Lots of them, actually.

Staple-gunned to the sitting-room wall were pages cut out from newspapers. Each one carried photos of me on fire, under screaming headlines like: CIRCUS HELL! THE DEVIL MADE ME DO IT! and: THE END OF THE WORLD IS AT HAND! There had to be at least thirty sheets from newspapers pinned to the walls of our flat. Five copies of the same front page titled HELL BREAKS LOOSE! circled the sitting room.

'Aidan,' Mimi cried, walking through the open front door and coming towards me, her arms outstretched. She gathered me into a hug. 'I just heard. I'm so sorry.'

Two police officers entered the flat with her.

'You and your mum are very welcome to stay with Sadie and me upstairs until your flat is sorted,' Mimi continued.

Which, with any luck, would be never. Swap our flat for the penthouse? Yes, please. Snooker room, here I come!

The two police officers came forward. They wanted my name, my details, who lived at the flat with me and Mum's work number. PC Furlong, a tall man with a square chin, said, 'I'm afraid I have some bad news too, son. It concerns your grandmother.'

His partner, a stern-faced woman with a broad nose called PC Odiah, said, 'It seems that, as the men who broke into your flat were leaving, your grandmother walked in on them.' She inhaled sharply. 'It appears there was a confrontation.'

I bet there was.

'Witnesses say your grandmother put up quite a fight,' PC Furlong said with a frown. 'Made it hard for them to escape. In the end, they bundled her into their van and drove away.'

It took a few moments for that to sink in. 'These burglars *kidnapped* Granny?'

PC Odiah's dark eyes softened. 'It's too early to say, but it does appear that way.'

'Don't you worry, son,' PC Furlong growled. 'We won't stop until we find these animals.'

I held a hand up. 'Honestly, officers. Take your time. There's no rush. In fact, a change of scenery might do Granny some good.'

PCs Furlong and Odiah stiffened. Their sympathetic gazes hardened and the atmosphere in the room became noticeably colder. Clearly, they'd mistaken Granny for a jolly grandmother, one who smiles whenever children enter a room and bakes apple tarts to pass the time.

As if.

The She-Bear, I explained to them, was not your average grandmother. Sadie and Hussein pitched in, Mimi too. Soon, a glimmer of recognition dawned on their stony faces.

'A walking stick, did you say?' PC Odiah licked the nub of her biro. 'Does your grandmother have a squint?'

'She does.'

'A little on the large side?' PC Furlong asked. 'Plays darts at The Anchor?'

'Wears her hair like a helmet?' PC Odiah questioned.

'Has a problem with pigeons?' PC Furlong queried.

'That's the one!' I said.

The two police officers exchanged a glance. 'We know her.'

PC Odiah crossed a line out in her notepad. Her stern face broke into a toothy grin. 'You may be right, son. A change of surroundings might do your grandmother a world of good.'

The questions didn't end there. Their attention turned to the break-in and these were harder to sidestep. The intruders were clearly searching for something, the officers said, but what?

'Does your mum keep anything valuable in here?' PC Furlong asked. 'Money? Jewellery?'

'No.'

'Well, we can discuss that with her. What about these?' PC Furlong tapped the newspaper stapled to the wall directly behind him. Its headline read: DEMON BURNS CIRCUS! 'The same story, over and over. These newspapers are a message.'

PC Odiah scowled. 'They look like a threat to me.'

I studied the photo of me rising out of the vaulting box covered in flames. 'Who would want to threaten me?'

A phone conversation later that afternoon:

Aitkens: (*Suspiciously*) Hello?

Me: It's me. Aidan.

Aitkens: (*A pause*) This is a surprise. How did you manage to get this number?

Me: That's for me to know and you to find out. Someone broke into my

	flat. Know anything about it?
Aitkens:	Have they? I am *so* sorry. You and your mum weren't hurt, were you?
Me:	No.
Aitkens:	A nasty business, break-ins.
Me:	Tell me about it. Everything we own is shredded or in pieces.
Aitkens:	Tsk, tsk, tsk. What a pity. And your grandmother? How is she?
Me:	Kidnapped, it seems.
Aitkens:	*(In an angry voice, as if speaking to someone nearby)* Kidnapped? What were they thinking when they took *her*? That doesn't sound like part of the plan! *(More quietly)* Tell me. How is your cat holding up?
Me:	My cat?
Aitkens:	I noticed you had one when I visited last week. Cats don't like surprises. Makes them nervous.
Me:	*(Speaks to Sadie and Hussein with hand over phone)* Have either of you seen Lemon?
Aitkens:	A nervous cat often runs away.

Me: Lemon isn't here. *(Bitterly)*
Neither is her cat box.

Aitkens: How strange. I hate it when things
go missing, don't you?

Me: Do you have Lemon?

Aitkens: Lemon? The fruit?

Me: Don't mess about. Do you have my
cat or not?

Aitkens: I must say, I don't like your
tone . . . but I do know a man who
can help. He's good at finding lost
cats.

Me: *(Angrily)* Lemon's not lost!

Aitkens: Things get lost all the time.
Don't they, Aidan? Things that are
important to people. I'll ask my
man to have a nose around for your
cat. I'd better warn you though.
He's expensive. It's going to cost
you.

Me: Cost me?

Aitkens: Yes. I believe you know *exactly*
what I want, and no tricks this
time. No fakes. I've got to hand

it to you. *(Laughs)* You surprised
me. Yes, you did! But I'm tired of
playing games. Understand? Or it
won't be just your cat and
grandmother who go missing next.

Me: *(Hesitantly)* Okay.

Aitkens: What's that? What did you say?

Me: I said 'okay'. I'll give you the
sweets – but I want Lemon *and*
Granny in exchange, and if
anything has happened to them, I
swear I'll burn you and the jar.

Aitkens: Don't worry. Your cat and
grandmother are safe. I'll give
you my word on that.

Me: *(No answer)*

Aitkens: I'll arrange for a car to pick you
up and bring you here.

Me: No. I'm not getting in any car you
send. Come to the circus tonight.
You bring Lemon and Granny, I'll
bring the sweets.

Aitkens: The circus? No way. Too many eyes
on us there.

Me: There won't be. The circus is
            closed. We'll have the Big Top to
            ourselves.

Aitkens: Are you certain that no one else
            will be there?

Me: No one. If the circus is closed,
            the performers won't leave their
            caravans. There won't be anybody
            about.

Aitkens: This had better not be another
            trick. My boys are armed. If they
            see one of those circus freaks
            nosing around they have orders to
            shoot on sight. Got it?

Me: Got it.

Aitkens: The circus it is, then. You have
            one hour. Six o'clock. Come alone.
            And Aidan, no fireworks,
            understand? Leave the flames at
            home – or you won't see your cat
            or your grandmother again.

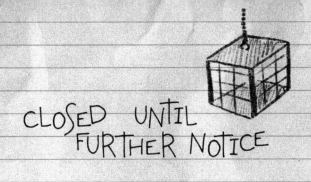

CLOSED UNTIL FURTHER NOTICE

At the entrance to the Heath, there was a banner taped over the Zarathustra's Travelling Circus billboard: CLOSED UNTIL FURTHER NOTICE. I ignored it and carried on up the footpath.

At the chain-link fence, two men in army jackets stopped me. Each of them wore a protective vest and carried a rifle.

'I'm here to see Ash Aitkens.'

The taller one pulled a radio out of his jacket and spoke into its mouthpiece. 'He's here.'

There was a pause as he listened to the reply.

'Yeah. He's alone.'

The guard put the radio down and stepped aside. 'They're waiting for you in the circus tent.'

I walked on.

A large white van was parked outside the Big Top. Two men, also in army jackets with rifles strapped to their shoulders, stood behind it. Otherwise, the circus was deserted. The neon signs beside Mathilde's caravan were dark. A large drop cloth covered the carousel, and there was no noise coming from the caravans stationed at the rear of the grounds. The circus seemed deserted.

I ducked behind the carousel to avoid being seen by the two men by the van. From there, it was a short walk to the costume caravan and the locker. Setting the numbers into place, I opened the lock.

One jar of Nature's Own.

Seven mints.

I took a deep breath. There was still time to walk away. Sadie had said I could. There was no guarantee our plan would work. But it was too late for second-guessing now. I removed the jar of Nature's Own and walked towards the Big Top.

The two guards by the van were waiting for me. 'What took you so long?' one said.

I lifted the jar of sweets. 'I had to pick this up.'

Their eyes widened. Though night had fallen, the fading light could not hide the greed etched into their faces, the desire curdling their hearts.

I gripped the jar tighter and hurried past them.

324

It was pitch-black inside the Big Top. I stumbled forwards in the dark, tempted to ignite one hand and use fire to light the way, but afraid of what might happen to Lemon if I broke my promise. Slowly, I edged nearer the centre ring.

A spotlight switched on. In the middle of the ring, a metallic folding chair became visible, illuminated by a narrow beam of white light.

Next came the loudspeaker.

'Sit in the chair,' boomed Ash Aitkens' voice.

I'm not going to lie. My knees were shaking as I made my way to that chair.

I sat.

'Put the jar of sweets on the ground.'

'No,' I said, speaking into the dark. 'Show me Lemon and Granny first.'

Two more spotlights flicked on. One revealed Granny inside the tall cage – a souvenir from the days when Zarathustra the bear travelled with Dmitri and the circus from town to town. The other spotlight was aimed at a seat in the third row where Lemon sat, locked inside her travel crate.

Granny blinked in the glare. 'Boy? Is that you?'

'Don't worry. Granny. I'll get you out of here

soon.' Shielding my eyes, I called out to Ash. 'I have what you want. Let my cat and grandmother go.'

The loudspeaker rumbled. 'Put the jar on the ground, first.'

'No.' I cradled the jar against my chest. 'Give me Lemon or this jar goes up in flames.'

There was a long pause.

The loudspeaker snarled, 'Free the cat.'

One of Aitkens' men opened the clips on the travel cage and Lemon bounded free. Scampering up the steps to the ring, she curled herself around my legs and purred.

'Granny next,' I said.

'No,' the voice from the loudspeaker boomed. 'Your turn. Put the sweets down. Then we let the old woman go.'

A voice inside my head went off like a siren, warning me not to do it, begging me to burst into flames and fly away while I had the chance. So much could go wrong. This might be my last chance to walk out of the Big Top alive.

I didn't give into temptation. I held my nerve. I placed the jar under my chair.

A man in a grey top shuffled down the aisle.

I assumed he was headed towards Granny's cage to free her.

He wasn't.

I didn't see the firehose until it was too late. Water hit me in the chest, blasting me off my feet. I skidded backwards across the ring. My head banged against a metal barrier and everything went dark.

not going to plan

I woke to find my wrists and ankles handcuffed to the metallic chair. Water dripped from my nose and chin. Thick layers of fire-extinguisher foam covered my chest, legs and hands. Overhead, a blinding white spotlight shone down on me.

And Ash Aitkens was standing right in front of me.

'Thought you could outfox me, didn't you, Sweeney?' Aitkens sneered. 'Fool!' Aitkens held up the jar of Nature's Own and shook it, rattling the mints inside. 'Once I swallow one of these capsules, I will show you what real power is!'

I tried to flame on – one fireball would wipe that smirk off Aitkens' face – but I had no flames, not even a spark, I was wet and miserable and utterly defeated. Handcuffed to the chair, I had no choice but to listen to this miserable rotter while he lorded it over me.

Aitkens unscrewed the lid and plucked two mints out of the jar. 'If a small turd like you can fly, imagine what powers will be granted to me.' He strutted around the ring like a mad peacock, his scrawny chest pumped out, his head back. 'Gather round! See history in the making! Witness the next step in human evolution!'

It was hard to tell which was worse – being handcuffed to a chair or listening to this waffle.

Aitkens' gang, on the other hand, looked like a bunch of fanboys at a movie première. They trooped closer, snapping pictures with their phones. The whole lot of them even gathered for a selfie around Ash with the two mints dangling over his mouth. To my right, Granny rattled her cage and shouted gruesome threats. Lemon remained near my feet, spitting and hissing at Aitkens whenever he came near.

Aitkens nibbled the jellied frosting off the mints until only the capsules were left. 'Ten months,' he said softly. 'Ten months of cosying up to Sloane. Ten months stuck in the village that time forgot. And now, finally, victory is here.'

I gulped.

This was NOT what we planned.

Where were they? Sadie and Hussein were supposed to be here. We did NOT want Aitkens anywhere near those sweets. But now it was too late.

Defeated, my chin slumped forwards as Aitkens popped both capsules into his mouth and began to chew.

'*Two* capsules,' I gasped. 'B-b-but you can't do that!'

Aitkens threw back his head and laughed. 'Rules are for cowards and sheep – not men like me. Yes, little Sweeney, I swallowed two drops, so watch and learn. You may think you are a fiery hero, but soon I will be TWICE as strong and TWICE as powerful!'

MONKEY business

The two capsules worked quickly.

Aitkens screamed.

He dropped to his knees. Clawed at his skin. He rolled about on the ground, crying in pain, and undergoing the most astonishing transformation before my very eyes.

Spikes of brown hair sprouted from his skin, some in thick lumps, others in patches of fine fur.

His hands and fingers lengthened and grew.

His feet burst out of his shoes.

His arms lowered, stretching until they almost reached the floor.

His face flattened. His beady eyes became dark and round; his lips turned black; his nose widened and changed colour, drooping over his face like a shrivelled blue cucumber. He cried and shrieked. He blubbered and sobbed. He beat the ground.

In fairness, it did look pretty painful. His guards backed away from him in horror, clearly unsure of what to do or how to help.

The only person not terrified was Granny. Clapping her hands, she cheered on every cry and groan. 'More! More!' she shouted, shaking the bars of her cage. 'Make him hurt!'

Staggering to his feet, Aitkens wrapped his long, hairy arms around his bottom and howled, his face contorted in pain. He spun round, unsteady on his large hairy feet, providing us with a good view of his new limb – a thick brown tail, curling out of his butt.

Throwing his head back, Ash Aitkens howled. He bared his yellow monkey teeth and hopped from foot to foot on his bandy legs.

If this was the next step in human evolution, god help us all.

A stunned silence fell over the men Aitkens had hired, a silence rudely broken by Granny's great peals of laughter. The old girl was beside herself.

I chose instead a moment of quiet reflection.

Aidan Sweeney's silent prayer of thanksgiving:
Thank you for granting me the self-control not to
gobble down another sweet, though every night
before bed, I dearly wanted to.

Aitkens didn't dance for long. Swivelling his hips
and slapping the ground with his long arms, he
raced to the centre post and up he climbed, to its
very top. From there, he sprang into the air,
swinging off ropes and trapezes as he sped from
one end of the Big Top to the other. He moved so
fast that he was a blur – on top of the bleachers one
moment, at the other end of the circus tent the next.
Leaping from one pole to the next, he finished by
somersaulting twice in the air and landing beside
me.

'I FEEL INCREDIBLE!' Aitkens shouted. He
walked back and forth in front of his gang like a
fashion model. 'What do you think, lads? How do
I look?'

His gang glanced nervously at each other.

'Uh . . . well, boss . . .' one started.

'It's – it's – it's different,' another tried.

'Forget to shave this morning, Monkey Boy?'

Granny cackled. 'Have a look in a mirror. You're in for a surprise!'

Stroking the fur on his face and neck, alarm began to dawn in Aitkens' black eyes. Then he stiffened. 'Do you hear that?' he cried nervously.

'Hear what, boss?' a shaven-headed man said.

Hackles raised, Aitkens turned towards the door, his big blue nose sniffing the air, as the doors to the Big Top burst open.

It was the Krazy Kar.

Travelling at high speed down the aisle, it skidded to a stop at the edge of the ring, tyres churning in the gravel. Its doors opened and out jumped Hussein and Sadie.

'You took your time getting here,' I said.

Sadie held up her palm, five fingers spread wide. 'Aidan, you do *not* want to go there.'

Let us leave our dashing hero handcuffed to a chair for one moment and travel back in time thirty minutes or so.

While I was entering the Big Top, Sadie and Hussein were approaching Zarathustra's Circus from the west – namely, walking up the short path leading to Mathilde's caravan.

Our plan? While I was diverting attention in the Big Top, Sadie and Hussein were to rouse the circus performers – specifically, Dead-Eye (and her six guns), the Kerrigan brothers (plus any/all of their instruments of destruction) and Atlas (with instructions to seek out Ash Aitkens and smash him repeatedly as hard as he possibly could) – so that we could storm the Big Top, rescue Lemon and Granny and defeat the forces of evil.

Unfortunately, it didn't work out that way.

A man had stopped Sadie and Hussein before they entered the caravan enclosure. Go home, he told them. The circus was closed. He also inquired why Hussein was carrying a plastic lightsabre in his hands (a good question). Hussein tried to engage the man in polite conversation. Sadie, however, preferred a more time-conscious approach. Using her telekinetic powers, she lifted him into the air and slammed him off Mathilde's caravan. As he slumped to the ground, our two heroes entered the caravan circle.

Here is where it began to go wrong.

Knowing the layout of the caravan enclosure, Sadie raced to Dmitri's caravan with Hussein hot on her heels. Throwing open his door, she shouted his name. Dmitri did not respond. Instead, he sat slumped in his chair, mouth open and snoring. They tried to rouse him. Shouts, shaking, slaps, water and threats were used. Nothing worked.

They tried another caravan.

Kenise 'the Cat' Williams and her children lived next door. Like Dmitri, Kenise (and her children) were asleep. Nothing could wake them.

They tried another caravan. No matter how hard

they tried, Atlas slept and slept and slept. Aware that a pattern was developing, Hussein made an important discovery. He noticed an unusual fruity smell (like spiced mango) inside the caravan, a scent that clung to Atlas – just as it had to Kenise and Dmitri. Could this smell explain why no one would wake?

Yes, it could.

The Mulungu tree grows in the rainforests of Brazil and Peru. By mixing its bright orange flowers with preparations made from its bark and roots, our scientists are transforming one of nature's most powerful sleep remedies into a highly effective tranquillizer.

Using drops of Mulungu oil (available over the counter from Cambio Laboratories Inc.), Ash Aitkens and his men had sprayed a sleep agent into each circus caravan shortly after their arrival.

No one from Zarathustra's Travelling Circus would be storming the Big Top tonight.

Late and growing desperate, Sadie and Hussein charged towards the Big Top. Already, blood-curdling screams could be heard from inside the circus tent. Aware that the entrances were watched, they halted behind the carousel, an opportunity for Sadie to assess their position and for Hussein to take a much-needed break from all this running.

It was here, while leaning against a smiling, green-tailed mermaid, that Hussein spotted the Krazy Kar parked beside the Ring-Toss. Opportunity beckoned! A chance to save the day *and* drive a stunt car! Off he ran to the Krazy Kar, Sadie close behind him. Hot-wiring the starter with a mere touch of his electro-fingers, Hussein wheeled round the carousel and sped towards the Big Top, hitting the doors at full throttle and into the next part of our adventure.

And now, back to our story.

hammer time

On one side of the centre ring were: Hussein, waving a plastic lightsabre; the Krazy Kar; Sadie with her arms outstretched in a warrior pose; me, handcuffed to a chair and covered in white foam; Lemon, licking her paw; and Granny, locked inside a bear cage, grinding her teeth, one eye twitching madly.

On the other side were: five square muscular men in camouflage clothing and army boots carrying automatic rifles; and one man-monkey admiring his tail in a mirror.

Sadie ran towards me. 'I'll get you out, Aidan.'

'No!' I shouted. The men in camouflage kit were creeping steadily down the aisles with their guns raised. 'Forget about me. Free Granny!'

Hussein placed his hand on the Krazy Kar and its boot opened.

Up came Sadie's hand. Out of the boot came the Kerrigan brothers' giant sledge-hammer. It whirled through the air like a tomahawk, crashing into the cage door and smashing the lock open.

Granny emerged, eye-twitching, arms flexing. She picked up the giant sledgehammer.

Running her hand down its long handle towards its mighty iron top, she shivered. A fierce gleam flickered across her face as she swung the giant sledge-hammer around her head like a whip. 'Who wants some of this?' she roared.

Her war-cry startled Ash Aitkens who scampered across the ring as fast as his bandy legs could take him. 'What are you waiting for?' he shouted at his men. 'Shoot them!'

They drew their guns.

Sadie countered. The rifles flew out of the men's hands and landed – in a neatly stacked pile, no less – in the boot of the Krazy Kar.

Aitkens glared at me. 'She has powers too? You GAVE the girl a mint? Are you mad? Do you know how much those capsules are worth?'

He pulled his hair.

He scratched his armpits.

He raced around the centre pole shrieking and hooting. I didn't have a handbook on monkeys on me but my guess was that Ash Aitkens was not a happy baboon.

Leaping from rope to rope, he landed on the top trapeze tier and shouted down at his men. 'Take them down! All of them!'

A burly man in a thick vest rushed across the ring towards Hussein. Hussein waved him off, swinging his plastic lightsabre at him.

'Do not underestimate my power.'

'Beat it, kid,' the man hissed. 'I don't have time for games.' He grabbed hold of Hussein's lightsabre.

CRACK!

A blast of light sent the man flying. When he stood up, white streaks dotted his smoking black hair and one of his eyebrows was missing.

'What happened?' I said. 'It looks like he was hit by a bolt of lightning.'

'He was.' Hussein swished his plastic lightsabre from side-to-side. 'Manipulate the ions inside eight AA batteries and you create an electromagnetic impulse.'

'Is there anyone you *didn't* give powers to?' snarled Ash from his perch.

'Good one, Hussein!' I cheered.

Sadie, meanwhile, had teamed up with Granny. The She-Bear led the attack, scattering Ash's men as they leapt out of the way of the sledge-hammer, while Sadie swept up behind, chucking the guards left and right with her power. Aitkens' gang didn't stand a chance.

Granny gathered the unconscious bodies of Aitkens' men and flung them towards the centre pole. Sadie did the rest, pulling the forgotten firehose through the air and wrapping it round them four times in a tight bow.

From the top of the Big Top, Aitkens howled.

'Give up!' Sadie shouted at him. 'Surrender now and you won't get hurt!'

How he laughed.

Scampering down the pole, he sneered at Sadie. 'Do you really think you can frighten ME?'

He raced from the pole to the prop box and opened it. Dipping his long arms inside, he hurled whatever he could find at us – juggling sticks, wrenches, hoops, cans and more. Sadie, Hussein and Granny batted them away with their sabre, hands and sledge-hammer, but they kept coming. Aitkens was insanely strong and his throws fierce and accurate.

He leapt on to the box and taunted them, howling and scratching his armpits. Aitkens could see they were tiring.

He wasn't though.

He was SO fast – a blur of hands and legs racing from one side of the Big Top to another. Sadie never stopped trying to snare him in her telekinetic grip, but he was too monkey-quick.

Round and round the centre ring he raced.

To the left of us.

Above us.

In the VIP seats.

On top of the bear cage.

Bouncing on the hood of the Krazy Kar.

Behind Sadie and Hussein, a red cloth in each paw.

Slapping the cloths over their mouths, he bared his teeth and hissed as their eyelids fluttered and closed.

'NO!' I cried, but it was no use. Sadie and

Hussein fell, curling next to each on the ground, asleep.

Granny aimed her sledge-hammer at Aitkens and threw, but missed.

Somersaulting over her head, Aitkens landed behind her, his legs recoiling like a spring on impact with the floor.

Thump!

A fierce kick in the back caught Granny by surprise. She slid forward and didn't get up.

Aitkens did.

He sauntered towards me. Then he pulled my head back with his furry paw. 'It's just you and me now, Sweeney.'

it's been nice knowing you

Ash Aitkens jingled the handcuff keys in my ear.

'Don't worry,' he snarled. 'You won't have to sit in this chair much longer.'

Laughing, he crumpled the keys into a twisted ball of metal and dropped them on the ground.

'What did you do to my friends?' I cried.

'Them?' He glanced over at Sadie and Hussein. 'They're asleep. A little whiff up the nose and off to dreamland.' He placed a hand over his heart and grinned. 'Trust me. It will be so much easier for them this way.'

My heart skipped. I could feel the hairs on my arm standing on end. 'What does that mean?'

Aitkens hooted and howled and laughed in my face. 'You know exactly what it means,' he sneered.

Don't cry, I told myself. *Don't cry. Don't give him the satisfaction.*

I'd almost forgotten about Lemon. She wasn't backing down either. She sprang at the monkey man, claws raised, catching him across the side of his face. She got a kick for her pains.

'Leave my cat alone!' I shouted.

Aitkens slapped the back of my head. 'Shut up, you. I give the orders.'

He raced over to the loudspeaker stand and returned with a blue gym bag, which he plonked on my lap. He unzipped it. The jar of Nature's Own was inside, along with a pair of socks and eight bundles of dynamite.

'No peeking,' he smirked, tapping my head.

Holding a bundle of dynamite in one hand, he bounded to the centre pole and climbed to the half-way stage. 'The army taught me a thing or two about explosives,' he said. 'When this goes off . . . *ka-boom*!' He threw back his head and howled. Hanging from his tail, he sealed the dynamite to the platform and set its timer.

His men had woken and were watching him in horror. They called to him, begging him to free them from the firehose.

He laughed in their faces. 'Goodbye, boys!' he

hooted. 'Sorry to disappoint you, but I've never been much of a team player. I prefer to work alone. You see, that way you don't have to share the profits.'

Aitkens raced down the pole and trotted towards me, his long arms trailing on the ground. 'I would love to stay and watch you die, Sweeney, but there are some caravans that need burning to the ground.'

He threw the blue gym bag over his shoulder. 'So long,' he laughed. 'When you meet your dad, tell him I said thanks.' He bared his teeth and hooted. 'Isn't life wonderful?'

action man

It's hard to explain what happened next. To be honest, I'm not sure myself. All I know is that when I saw Sadie, Hussein and Granny fighting back, deep down inside I felt a spark.

It began to grow.

When Ash Aitkens tied the dynamite to the platform, the spark had become a fierce flame.

When Lemon scratched Aitkens' face? Hotter.

The goodbye to his mates, his supposed friends who he abandoned and left to die? The flame grew hotter still.

When I realised that he was going to burn down the circus caravans with Dmitri, Mathilde, Eshe, Rodrigo and everyone else inside them? MUCH hotter.

As for leaving Sadie and Hussein and Lemon and even Granny to die, well . . . not while I had breath in my body.

I exploded.

My handcuffs melted off.

The foam evaporated. The chair shattered.

The force of the blast flung Ash Aitkens to the ground.

I shot into the air and ripped the dynamite from the platform. Hugging it close to my flaming chest, it exploded.

BOOM!

As you might have guessed by now, thinking ahead has never been one of my strengths. Strategy and planning is Sadie's department. Hussein handles the explanations. I'm the action hero, so don't ask me what happened, but somehow my body absorbed the energy from the blast. The Big Top shook. Its canvas stretched like a great balloon, lifting into the air and almost tearing the circus tent from its pegs.

But the only person hurt was me.

I fell.

The dynamite's shock waves were too powerful for me to control. They overwhelmed my flames and flung me backwards. I hit the ground hard, skidding across the gravel until I rolled to a stop. Legs cut, bruised and battered, my clothes burnt off, I was fairly content to lie there and do nothing for quite some time.

An angry man-monkey had other ideas.

Aitkens lifted me off the ground by my neck.

'FOOL!' he roared, shaking me like a rag doll. 'Look what you've done!'

In his other hand was a broken jar of Nature's Own.

'They're gone! GONE! Melted! Destroyed by you and your fire! Do you know how much those capsules were worth? BILLIONS!' Aitkens bared his yellow teeth and howled. 'You miserable, interfering idiot! You don't *deserve* powers!'

'And you do?

'YES!' The monkey man snarled, so furious with me that he didn't notice the large old woman rising behind him. 'I understand the potential of real power!'

'No you don't. You've never understood what real strength is.'

His grip tightened around my throat. He hissed and hooted, chomping his teeth.

'Real strength is other people,' I said. 'It's your friends. It's working together to help others, not yourself. Isn't that right, Granny?'

Ash Aitkens stopped hissing. 'Granny?' He blinked.

KAPOW!

Ash Aitkens, say hello to Granny's giant sledge-hammer.

the finale

One by one, the circus crew woke and stumbled into the smoking Big Top.

They were greeted by a strange sight. Three rows of seats were melted, scorch marks streaked the canvas tent and the centre-post was now charcoal-black. The lid of the prop box had been ripped open and its contents strewn across the ring. The Krazy Kar was parked at an odd angle and its hood badly dented. Six sorry thugs were tied to the centre-post with a fire hose and a wide-set old woman with one eyebrow, a twitchy eye and a giant sledge-hammer over her shoulder was standing guard over a monkey-man chained to Zarathustra's bear cage.

Dmitri was first in. Rubbing his whiskers, he did a slow circuit of the Big Top. He inspected the tent and pole. He nodded at the bound men and stopped to stare at the monkey man inside his bear cage.

Finally, he shuffled back where I waited, a fire blanket tucked round me.

'You've been busy,' he said.

i Spy

Dmitri rang the police. When PCs Furlong and Odiah arrived, they took one look at Ash Aitkens – the monkey arms and legs, his bright blue (and now very flat) nose, his fur and tail – and immediately went to make a call.

'Identifying *this* creature is well above my pay grade,' PC Odiah told us.

A tall, grey-haired man arrived in a black sedan. He wore a rumpled navy suit and a smart pink tie. Three agents in uniforms followed him as he strolled into the Big Top. He took a keen interest in the singed markings on the canvas – sniffing it at one stage – and in the melted seats. He circled the bear cage twice before approaching Ash Aitkens, the three agents at his heel.

PC Furlong snapped to attention. 'Sir!'

'At ease, officer.' The agent peered into the cage. 'Well, hello!' he cried. 'What do we have here?'

Crouched on the ground, his long hairy arms

wrapped around his ears, Ash Aitkens sulked. No longer brash, no longer bragging, he was a shadow of the monkey he once was, stewing in silence.

The agent tapped the metal bars. 'Come on, old boy. This is no time to be shy, Mr Aitkens! My colleagues and I have been looking forward to meeting you. We've been keeping a close eye on you since your misadventures in South America.'

Inside the cage, Aitkens scratched his butt, then sniffed it.

'How interesting.' He turned to PC Furlong. 'Am I to believe that is *not* a costume he has on?'

'No sir,' said PC Furlong. 'That's proper fur he's got on. PC Odiah and I got a right shock when we tried to take his tail off.'

'I can only imagine,' the agent said. 'Has he said much?'

PC Odiah squinted through the bars at Ash Aitkens. 'He nattered a bit when we first arrived, but he's said nothing since.'

'Licking his wounds, no doubt,' the agent said. Noticing the crowd of circusfolk, he smiled. 'Allow me to introduce myself. My name is Russell R Whittaker.' He flashed us a badge. 'MI5.'

Dmitri shook his hand.

Sadie, Hussein and I gazed at the MI5 agent from behind Dmitri. He nodded, smiling at us as his keen brown eyes swept over us. 'Good evening.'

'Do you know what happened to him?' Sadie asked, glancing at the man-monkey squatting on the ground.

'Our people in South America have filed a report about a tree in Machu Picchu which bears the most remarkable fruit. It seems a laboratory tried to harvest it. Aitkens and an associate of his got wind of this and tried to steal it for themselves.' Agent Whittaker bent nearer to the three of us, as if he were going to pass on a secret. 'I may be wrong,' he whispered, 'but I get the very distinct feeling that you already know this.'

From inside the cage, Ash Aitkens growled at the three agents who had arrived with Agent Whittaker and were filming him. 'Go away, all of you! Leave me alone! You're giving me a headache.'

'The monkey speaks!' Agent Whittaker laughed. 'Excellent! I have the proof I came for.' He turned the three officers. 'You can shoot him now.'

They undid their jackets. Holsters were strapped across their chests.

Ash Aitkens sprang to his feet, his hackles high. 'Hold on. Did you say, *shoot me?*'

The agents aimed their pistols.

'Don't! Stop! Wait! Please, I'll tell you everything you want to know!'

'Yes, you will, old boy. Yes, you will.' Agent Whittaker nodded. The three agents raised their pistols.

'STOP! PLEASE!' Aitkens howled.

Three darts hit him in the chest and, for the second time that evening, down he went.

See no evil, hear no evil

Covering his face with a hood, the police strapped Aitkens to a stretcher and wheeled him into an unmarked van. Ash Aitkens, we learned, would be taking up new lodgings deep in the basement of MI5, where he would be certain to keep guards, scientists, the jungle gym and barbers busy for the foreseeable future.

PC Furlong chuckled. 'Don't worry. No one will be seeing that lad again.'

Agent Whittaker, however, wasn't finished with us. As the van containing Aitkens drove off, he pulled us aside.

'Tell me, did our hairy friend happen to mention a jar of sweets by any chance? I would be very keen to get my hands on it.'

I opened my mouth, but Dmitri stepped forward. 'I found this under blue bag.' He held out the empty shards of the Nature's Own jar. 'I put it to one side for police. Must be important, I think.'

Agent Whittaker could not hide his disappointment. 'Thank you, Dmitri.' He turned to one of the officers with him. 'Get what's left to the lab and tell them to send the results directly to me.'

As the van containing Ash Aitkens rumbled off, Agent Whittaker got into his sedan.

'Good day, children.' He smiled. 'I very much expect you will hear from me again.'

Mum

Mum arrived at the circus in a right state. As soon as she got out of the cab, I threw my arms around her and told her I was sorry. I had kept a secret from her, a big one, and that's when it all spilled out.

357

I told her the truth – about me and fire, the parcel, Ash Aitkens, everything. It wasn't easy, but I had to. I owed her that much.

Was she upset that I had turned myself into a flame-wielding superhero? No.

Was she hurt that I kept a secret from her? Yes.

I couldn't stop smiling now that the truth was out – though as Mum said, watching her son burst into flames would take some getting used to. You should hear her scream when I sneak up behind her with my head on fire!

the music box

We went upstairs to stay with Mimi and Sadie. There wasn't much to salvage from our flat, bits and pieces mostly. Ash Aitkens had destroyed nearly everything.

Though Dad's music box was in tatters, I couldn't leave it behind. I collected all the bits I could find and gave them to Dmitri. If anyone could restore it, he could. The man threw nothing away. The trailer behind his caravan was a home for broken lamps, bicycles, spotlights and Whack-a-Moles.

Nothing gave him more pleasure than finding a way to mend something broken and make it new again.

And, sure enough, Dmitri fixed it.

He and I made a big show of it, inviting Mum into his caravan for the great unveiling. It *was* a surprise too. You could never tell it had been cracked or repainted. Flip it open and the music played – better than before, as a matter of fact – and the drummer boy banged his drum.

But the biggest surprise was yet to come.

Dmitri said, 'Very clever box, this.' He picked it up and turned it over. 'It has hidden lock.'

Mum leaned in for a closer look. 'What do you mean?'

'The music is for show. This is magic box. Use to hold secrets.' He tapped a lever at the bottom and out popped a small spiral notepad with the smallest, elf-like handwriting. It was Dad's diary, filled with letters home that he'd written but never sent, bits of writing he kept, funny stories, the odd poem. Mum cried and laughed and kissed and thanked us both.

'This is the best present *ever*!'

Later that night, when we were alone, she showed me a small page. It was about me.

You flopped out the way most babies do, your eyes closed and bawling. I keep a photo of newborn you in my wallet, so I can carry it everywhere. Your mum is there too, in a hospital gown, her hair long. I'm beside her, uniform on. You are wrapped in a blanket, a red-raw runt with tiny fists, your mouth open. Under it Mum wrote, 'Hello, World'.

I will never forget that day, you with wisps of red hair stuck to your head. Wrapped in white, you looked like a tiny candle. I knew then there could only be one name for you.

Aidan

It means 'fiery one'. It's an old name, Irish like my own, and comes from the Celtic god of the sun and fire, Aodh.

Wear it well, Aidan. Burn bright, son. Be kind. Fill the world with sunshine.

I love you.

hello Zarathustra's

After a few nights at Sadie's, Dmitri offered me and Mum the use of a caravan until our flat was ready. 'Use it. Stay a day. Stay a week, longer if you like.'

Mum accepted. She told me later it was the caravan's colour – a flaming orange-red – that had swayed her.

The day we moved in the whole circus lined up to welcome us. Dmitri invited Sadie and Hussein too and organised a barbecue in our honour. There were sausages, burgers, curried potatoes, grilled aubergines, spice-crusted tofu, corn on the cob and a small hog roast, which Atlas managed to tuck away himself, more or less. It was a blast. The caravan felt like home after that.

Sure, I'd miss climbing the fire escape to meet Sadie or riding the lift with Hussein, but visiting people wasn't a problem for a boy who could fly.

The circus suited Granny too.

Granny

Granny embraced circus life. She pumped weights with Atlas after breakfast, spat chew tobacco with

Dead-Eye in the afternoon and downed a vodka or two with Dmitri before dinner. Much of her spare time was spent terrorising the pigeons who dared land near the circus grounds or dropping in on her new best mates, the Kerrigan brothers. The clatters, thumps, clangs and rumbles coming from that caravan beggared belief.

The circus may have been the change of scenery Granny needed. She actually smiled at me the other day – a frightening sight, I have to admit. Her mouth wasn't used to twisting in that direction – but we were all pleased for her.

Best of all, Granny had her own digs. Dmitri helped Mum find a second-hand camper van, which they set up for her at the far end of the green.

Did I miss sharing a confined living space with Granny?

Not in the slightest.

Best of all, here were no more worries about closing the circus now. Dmitri said he owed it all to his brilliant new business plan.

Me.

be afraid. be very afraid.

The day after our big bust-up in the Big Top, Hussein uploaded a video on YouTube. In two hours, it had over three hundred hits. By the next day, it had three hundred _thousand_.

It opens with smoke as haunting music plays in the background. Fiery words form: _Be Afraid. Be Very Afraid._ The words burn away and the image is replaced with a clip of me on fire. It shows me in flames, rising out of the vaulting box. Noises from the crowd – gasps and screams, mostly – are heard.

As I ascend into the air, the screams get louder. Fiery words reappear: _ZARATHUSTRA'S TRAVELLING CIRCUS presents FIRE BOY. See him ... if you DARE._ The last shot is a wobbly, hand-held video of me flying over a frightened crowd. It ends with a link to a website and the words, _BOOK NOW._

Demand for tickets was so great that the circus squeezed more seats into the Big Top. They were already sold out for the next month, Dmitri said, and if _Fire Boy_ went well, Zarathustra's could stay in London for a year.

No pressure, then.

Lemon

Lemon didn't take to the circus at first. She wasn't herself from the moment we moved in. At first, we thought it was the change in routine or that she missed the flat. But each day she got worse and worse. She stopped going out. She wouldn't play. She even stopped eating. I was worried.

Then, one morning, I made a discovery. I found something under our bed. A tiny white bundle. I pulled it out cautiously, afraid it was a mouse, and instead found a half-chewed sock. Inside the sock I found a chunk of melted glass with four jellied mints attached to it.

I examined the sock and mints carefully.

It couldn't be. Could it?

Gently prising apart each mint, I found a tiny nut-shaped capsule hidden inside. Four mints! Four capsules! One was missing! Scrambling to the edge of the mattress, I dipped my head under the posts to see if I could find the other mint when the bed lurched suddenly as if something enormously heavy had jumped on to it. Sliding backwards, I fell into the flanks of a large ginger and white tiger.

The tiger roared.

'Lemon?'

Laying its head on my lap, the tiger purred and closed its eyes.

Well . . . this might take some getting used to.

Fire Boy flies again

From the back window of the caravan, you could see the queue. It stretched from the park gate to the High Street. Two TV vans were parked at the entrance, reporters interviewing people waiting to get in.

'Can you believe it?' Sadie said to me and Hussein. 'This is the hottest ticket in town. Everyone we know is here.'

She wasn't joking. Alice Laurel, Sadie's mum, had flown in from America and was already seated in one of the VIP boxes with Mum and Mimi. Hussein's mum, dad, two sisters, his younger brother, uncle, and grandparents were joining them too.

Agent Whittaker had bought a ticket for the show. 'Wouldn't miss it for the world!' he said.

Miss Spatchcock and Mr Henderson were in the crowd, with Joe Jackson, and most of Caversham

School – except for Mitchell Mulch. He swore he'd never set foot in a circus again, which was fine by me.

As we waited for the crowd to be seated, we played with Lemon – carefully, I should add; a tiger who still thinks she's a cat can break a lot of furniture inside a caravan – and chatted about the show, school and whether Arjun, a snake-charmer from Jaipur who Mathilde was seeing, might join the circus someday.

Suddenly, the carnival music stopped and the loudspeaker buzzed on.

'Ladies and gentlemen, boys and girls, please take your seats. This evening's performance of Zarathustra's World-Famous Travelling Circus, featuring FIRE BOY, is about to begin.'

It was time to put on my costume. 'Wait until you see this,' I said.

I opened my bag to show them a lava-red jersey and tights. 'Dmitri gave it to me. He says it will never burn away, no matter how hot I get.'

Hussein checked the label. 'Protecto-Wear? Wow! How did Dmitri get his hands on this?'

Protecto-Wear was top-of-the-line, military-grade,

flame-resistant clothing – the best in the business. Able to withstand the hottest and coldest temperatures known on earth. Hussein stroked the pair of red leggings. 'This must have cost a fortune.'

'He got it in Kiev.'

'But how did—'

'Dmitri said, "In Kiev street market, best not to ask questions." ' I ran my fingers over its lining. 'He said he couldn't have me flying around the tent with no clothes on.'

They laughed.

'That's a shame. I was hoping for a repeat of our assembly. What a showstopper that would be!' Hussein said.

'Ha, ha.'

'Put it on!' Sadie cried. 'Put it on!'

I went behind the dresser and slipped it on. The Protecto-Wear jersey had a hood with a small face mask. Dmitri had cut peek holes for eyes and added two little horns to its top. When I turned round, I found a tiny pointy tail attached to my bottom.

I put it on, walking up and down to whistles and shrieks from Sadie and Hussein.

'I so wish Mimi were here,' Sadie laughed. 'You finally nailed fancy dress.'

'Loving the tail. It suits you.' Hussein said.

I flicked the two horns sewed on my head and watched them wobble. 'Dmitri says I'm supposed to be an imp.'

'Imp?'

'A little demon. Like a naughty schoolboy, but from Hell.'

Sadie said, 'Perfect.'

'It's you, mate. It's you,' Hussein said.

We stepped out of the caravan as Dmitri boomed out the first lines of my intro over the loudspeaker.

'*ARE YOU READY?*

'*Brace yourselves, boys and girls, ladies and gentlemen.*'

Sadie and Hussein walked with me as I took my place outside the main entrance

'*Do you feel the heat? Do you see his smoke?*

'*It is time.*

'*FIRE BOY nears.*'

'Nervous?' Hussein asked.

'Very.'

They took my hands. 'Come on,' Sadie said.

'You can do this – and *only* you can do this, remember that.'

Dmitri had asked Mathilde to paint a special marker for me so I knew where to stand before I took off. It was hard to miss. It was a picture of the Fool – the Fool from the tarot cards – with these words running around it: '*A true friend walks in when the rest of the world walks out.*'

Tips on how to get along with others #4:
Being a good friend isn't easy, but it's always worth it.

Sadie held up a hand. The circus tent billowed and bent as its main doors flew open. Hussein placed his hand on the cable near the carousel and every light in the circus flared.

I ignited.

Shooting into the night sky, I zoomed over the Heath and twirled over the rooftops of Camden.

Dmitri's voice boomed over the speakers again.

'*Imprisoned beneath the pyramids of Egypt for over 3000 years, El Diablo is free and he is ... READY TO RUMBLE!*'

'On your feet, boys and girls.

'Start clapping, ladies and gentlemen.

'This is one little devil you do NOT want to insult!'

Banking around a cloud, I began a long, low descent, a tail of flames trailing behind me.

'FIRE BOY IS HERE!'

I flew through the main doors and entered the Big Top like a rocket.

WAIT!

DON'T CLOSE THE BOOK
JUST YET!

THERE'S MORE!

TURN THE PAGE
AND SEE

In the Burns Unit of Peru's *Hospital Regional de Callao*, a patient stirs. She reaches for the cup on her bedside table.

It's empty. She presses the call button beside her bed and waits.

No one comes.

Nurses never seem to come to Room 13. Not alone, at any rate.

Especially not at night.

The patient struggles out of bed. Carefully, she treads across the floor to the basin. Her bandaged limbs ache. After so many weeks in bed, the short walk exhausts her.

She fills a glass with water and drinks greedily, wetting her parched lips and dry, sticky mouth.

And then, a month and two days after sustaining severe injuries in an explosion at Cambio Laboratories,

Sloane Sixsmith sees her reflection in the mirror for the first time since the fire.

Her skin is covered in scales and vivid green in colour.

Her eyes are yellow.

Her mousy-brown hair is short and spiked. Streaks of white and lime run through it.

Feeling faint, Sloane places a hand against the wall to steady herself. Immediately, her reflection begins to alter. Her scales fade. Her hair lengthens into a curtain of tan and gold stripes. Her eye and skin colour change too, transforming into the same shades and stripes as her hair – and, she notices, the very same pattern of the wallpaper in Room 13.

Straightening, she lets go of the wall. She watches her hair shorten, her eyes turn yellow and her greenish scales return.

'This is interesting,' Sloane says aloud.

She grips the sink basin and sees her reflection go white. She picks up a sponge and her hair curls into an orange afro, while her skin bubbles and changes colour.

When she looks into the mirror for the final time

that night, Sloane Sixsmith is smiling.

At breakfast the next morning, the nurses on the Burns Unit check on 'the creature' in Room 13. When they enter her room, they discover she is gone. Her bandages lie heaped on the floor and her few possessions – sandals, a smock and a locket containing a heart-shaped photograph of herself and Ash Aitkens – are gone.

Sloane Sixsmith has a plane to catch.

CAN SLOANE 'THE CHAMELEON' SIXSMITH RESCUE ASH 'MONKEY MAN' AITKENS FROM A JAIL CELL IN THE BASEMENT OF MI5?

WILL GRANNY AND LEMON TURN HAMPSTEAD HEATH INTO A PIGEON-FREE ZONE?

WHAT NEW ADVENTURES AWAIT DMITRI, MATHILDE, ATLAS AND THE OTHER STARS OF ZARATHUSTRA'S TRAVELLING CIRCUS?

IS SADIE GOING TO STAMP OUT CRIME IN LONDON?

WILL HUSSEIN EVER LEARN HOW TO PLAY THE ELECTRIC GUITAR PROPERLY?

CAN AIDAN GO TWO WEEKS WITHOUT BURNING OFF HIS CLOTHES?

THE ANSWERS TO THESE QUESTIONS AND MUCH MORE AWAIT IN . . .

FIRE BOY'S NEXT BLAZING ADVENTURE

Coming soon!

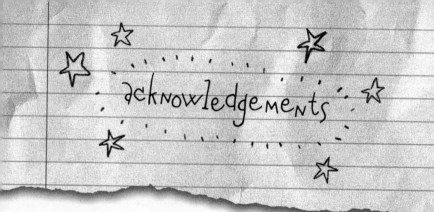

acknowledgements

It takes a lot of people to put a novel together. I was fortunate to have so many talented people helping me.

I could never have written *Fire Boy* without the world's greatest librarian, Jenny Jones, and her sons, Elliot and Sam. From the novel's first chapter, their support encouraged me to carry on. They stayed with me through draft after draft with tips, suggestions and feedback. Jenny, Elliot and Sam: Thank you so very much.

Becky Bagnell coaxed and prompted a manuscript into being. Is there a better agent anywhere? I doubt it.

Lena McCauley, my editor, should have her name alongside mine on the cover. She pinpointed what I needed to correct, edit, improve and cut with great patience and kindness.

Samuel Perrett's cover and brilliant illustrations lifted the novel to another level.

Ruth Alltimes, Dom Kingston, James McParland, the design team and proofreaders at Hachette – in fact, everyone I came in contact with there – were a joy to work with.

Genevieve Herr brought rigour and a few good jokes to a late draft. Emma Roberts picked over a final copy with great care and insight.

Students and lecturers at Bath Spa's MA Writing for Young People helped me with this novel, especially Julia Green, Jules Wilkinson, Lucy Tallis, Hilary Jelbert and Jo Pestel.

A special mention about Jo: Though Jo Pestel passed away before she could finish her own novel, her laughter and fierce passion for life will be remembered by all who knew her.

Alison Powell and her writing workshops in Bristol kept me going. Feedback from her and her fellow Write Clubbers was a godsend.

And finally, closer to home ...

To family and friends: The well wishes and encouragement meant a lot. Thank you.

To our dogs, Winnie and Rose: Good times

writing that novel, eh?

To Hannah, Conor and Ben: Be honest. You weren't expecting that, were you?

To Mags: We did it.